Forgetting

Going back to the house we fooled around, passing the basketball back and forth, arguing and yelling at each other. Uncle Paul and Aunt Joan were waiting for us in front of the house. Grandma Betty was sitting on the steps, leaning her head against the railing.

"Grandma!" Lori ran up to her. Just then the ball popped out of my arm and I ran into the street after it. "Billy!" Aunt Joan cried. "Be careful."

I stood in the street, ashamed because I was holding the basketball, ashamed because I had been playing and had forgotten everything.

**Other Point paperbacks
you will enjoy:**

point

WHEN THE PHONE RANG

Harry Mazer

SCHOLASTIC INC.
New York Toronto London Auckland Sydney

ISBN 0-590-40383-4

12 11 10 9 8 7 6 5 4 3   8 9/8 0 1/9

Printed in the U.S.A.   01

For the whole gang:
Sam Mazer, Jean Fox, and Andy and Max,
Sue and Jerry, Joe and Gina.

When The Phone Rang

Chapter 1

When the phone rang the first time that afternoon, I was home alone, lying on the living-room rug with the newspaper spread in front of me. The Christmas tree, I remember, was shedding all over the paper. It was nearly February, but we always kept our tree to the bitter end. The phone rang again. Too early for Mom and Dad. Their plane wasn't due in till later.

Getting to my feet I accidentally brushed a picture off the coffee table. The glass broke. *Great going.* Good thing it wasn't one of my mother's prize photos. She was a professional photographer. Her pictures were all over the house. The first thing she and Dad did when we moved here just before this last

Thanksgiving was convert the little bathroom off the kitchen into a darkroom.

When the A&P in Delmar closed down last year Dad lost his job. For nineteen years he'd been their chief warehouse foreman and there was no comparable job for him in the area. That's when they started talking about moving to the city. Lori and I were against it, but Mom said, "This is a big chance for your father." She wanted it, too. More photo assignments, more jobs, more opportunity, more everything. So we'd come to the Big City and Dad got a job with Empire Trucking. We'd been here almost four months now and they loved it, but I still wasn't used to the Big Wonderful City, or the Big Wonderful School I went to, or the Big Wonderful Street we lived on. Chained garbage cans, chained doors, dirty snow, no place to turn around. The playground had a ten-foot fence around it that they chained shut at night. In Delmar, I just went out of the house and I could ski down the street or go snowshoeing up in the hills. In Delmar — No! I'd promised myself I'd stop whining about Delmar.

The phone rang again. "Lori?" I said, picking it up in the kitchen. I pushed aside an open cracker box. My sister and I had been grubbing it all week while our parents were living it up in Bermuda. The company had flown all the big and little execs (Dad) and their mates down to the Caribbean on a combination midwinter business meeting and vacation.

"Lori?" I said again. She had promised to help me clean up the mess before they came.

2

"Bo?" It was a female voice, not my sister's.

"Bo who?"

"Comedian, get Bo. I want to talk to him."

She sounded like Kristy McNichol. "Maybe I can help," I said.

"How are you going to help? Bo, that moron, sent me the wrong order again."

"I don't see Bo right this minute," I said, squinting down the dark hall. I began to identify with the unknown Bo. It could have been me in the same fix. "Anybody can make a mistake."

"Do you know what you're talking about? That customer is here running around like a raging bull. We've had his car tied up in the yard for three weeks waiting for these parts. And now he's going to have to wait three more weeks. Who is this anyway?"

"Billy — "

"Billy? Where did you come from? Do I have the wrong number? I do, don't I?" And she hung up.

I picked up the picture I'd broken and put it back with the others. It was Kevin's high school graduation picture. My friend Lamby had taken it. In the picture Dad had his arm around Kevin, Mom had her arm around Lori, and I was behind all of them, two fingers raised above my brother's head.

Kevin had just walked off with the Outstanding Athletic Achievement Award, the Baylor Biology Prize, the American Legion's Good Citizenship Award, and the Latin Prize. Kevin was Super Achiever. I always had the idea that, if I wanted to enough, I could do anything, too. But so far nothing had seemed that important. Which was maybe why my father had this joke about me. "Billy has three speeds — slow, half slow, and stored for the winter."

Last year I had a growth spurt and I went out for football. I liked the contact, grabbing and banging heads, but I never took the game seriously, the way Kevin had. In one scrimmage — as it turned out, my last — the coach moved me from tackle to end, my brother's old position. In the play I had to swing around the defender, get in the clear, then cut for the center and look for the ball. I did that part all right, broke free, turned, and saw the ball coming. It was a perfect throw — a perfect miss, too. The ball went through my hands like they were the Grand Canyon. Well, maybe I shouldn't have laughed. End of football career.

I looked out the front windows. Dark and wintry. Passing cars winding around double-parked cars. Nothing to see but cars and the wall of blank-faced buildings on the other side of the street. Where was Lori? She was supposed to be home to help me clean up before Mom and Dad came back. I fingered the big Mercedes key in my pocket. The car had to be moved each day from one side of the street to the other. Maybe I'd drive around and look for her.

In the hall, Mrs. Stein was sweeping the stairs. She had arthritis in her fingers and held the broom awkwardly. "William, you left your lights on again. They were on all day when you were in school."

I wished my mother hadn't asked the Steins, who lived upstairs, to keep an eye on us while she and

4

Dad were away. Mrs. Stein took the job too seriously. When you were sixteen, it was humiliating to be watched and corrected every minute.

"I'm just going out for a sec. . . ." But then I went back and shut the lights.

Mrs. Stein followed me to the front door. "You also left the door unlocked. An open door is an invitation to trouble."

I didn't know how I could have done that. There were two big locks on the door that automatically snapped shut when you went out. "Sorry about that."

I went out, then tried the door from the outside. Older people worried too much, including my parents. The Steins had two locks on their door, plus a steel bar they set in place when they were inside. It didn't give me a lot of confidence in the city.

I walked toward South Avenue. The whole block was like one long attached house, brownstones, one next to the other, with high stone steps and iron railings across the front. There was a stink of coal and sulfur in the air. The few trees on the street were like half-dead scarecrows with sheets of plastic caught in their branches. The plan was, as soon as spring came the Kellers were going to plant a healthy tree in the square of mud in front of their house.

I'd parked the Mercedes on Seventy-ninth Street. Every time I went to get the car I was afraid that I'd find a rock through the windshield or the wheels missing. It was an old car but Dad kept it in perfect shape. It had never been left on the street till we moved here.

I drove the car slowly down the block, keeping an eye out for Lori. I could almost hear Dad say, *No tooting around. Just park the car.*

I'm not tooting around, Dad. I'm looking for Lori. She'd mentioned going to the Catholic Youth Organization on Dyer Avenue to play basketball so I drove that way. At every corner I slowed and beeped, hoping somebody — a girl — would look around and say, *Fantastic!* I'd give her the nod and she'd jump in the car. It was one of my few good fantasies about the city. There were a lot more girls here than in Delmar, but they were a lot harder to meet.

The CYO was in a yellow brick building that smelled like old sweat socks. The gym was downstairs. Behind the double doors I heard the dull, underwater thud of basketballs.

Lori was down at the end, playing basketball with three girls. She was wearing my faded red sweat shirt. The girl guarding Lori was a lot bigger, but clumsy. She kept rushing at Lori and throwing up her arms. Lori was smooth, passed the ball to her partner, then blocked her opponent. "Shoot, Sam," she yelled, "shoot over her."

She was crowing when she quit. She came up holding Sam's hand. "Did you see the way that fat Elaine kept pushing into me?" She fanned herself with her braids. "What are you doing here, Billy? My brother," she said. Sam was tall and round-faced, a nice face. Cute.

Sam checked me out. I smiled and pushed Lori toward the stairs. "Remember we agreed to clean up before Mom and Dad came back?"

6

"We'll do it. You don't have to act like a dictator."

Outside I gave her a ten-second lead, then raced her to the car. She got there a step ahead of me.

"Beat you."

"Next time, no lead."

"Excuses. You didn't even count to ten. What are you puffing about? Is that the way you breathe normally? You're getting to be an old man, William."

I parked the car in front of the house, lucky to find a spot. "Who's the girl, the tall one, your partner?"

"Sam. You like her?"

"Just asking. She's not as good as you are."

"You like her! Oh, William, you like a girl."

"Will you stop bellowing like an idiot?" My sister didn't know what quiet was. She talked, pushed — she didn't like to be left out of anything. From the first day we moved here, she had friends.

"You do like her. Sam's got it." Lori put her hand to her chest. "I know what you're thinking. You're blushing! Don't act so innocent."

"You've got a big mouth. I'm not interested in your young friends."

"Young friends! Listen to the old man. Wait'll you see my other friend, Maryanne. You won't think she's so young."

7

Chapter 2

A phone was ringing as we came up the stairs. "Is that our phone?"

"I'll get it." Lori raced up the stairs with me behind her.

"If it's Mom and Dad at the airport we're in trouble."

"Hello. . . ." Lori had the phone in the hall and was smiling expectantly the way she always did when she answered the phone. "Yes, yes." She nodded. "This is the Keller house. Who do you want? What? Joe Keller?" She put her hand over the phone. "They want to talk to the person in charge." She pointed to herself.

I snatched the phone. "Hello, this is Billy Keller." I deepened my voice. "Can I help you?"

"This is Pan-Con Air," a woman said. "I'd like to talk to the person in charge."

"Yes. . . ."

"Who is this?"

"Billy Keller. Have my parents' flight plans been changed?"

"Are you a relative of Joseph Keller?"

"Yes, I'm his son. What is it?"

"I'm calling about a charter flight from Bermuda to Miami. There are a Joseph and Phil Keller on the passenger list."

"Phyllis Keller," I corrected her. "They should be in Miami now, boarding another plane home."

There was a hesitation on the other end of the line, silence, then the hum of distant wires. I wondered where she was calling from.

"This is the home of Joseph and Phil Keller?"

"Phyllis Keller," I repeated.

She spelled the names, then repeated the address. "Is there somebody else there? Somebody older?"

"What is it? Who do you want?"

"Look, I have something hard to tell you. . . . Your parents' plane . . . Charter Flight 45 crashed into the Caribbean at four-twenty this afternoon. There were — "

I hung up abruptly.

The phone rang again almost immediately. It was the woman again. "We were cut off," she said. "I'm sorry — Charter Flight 45 crashed into the Caribbean at four-twenty this afternoon. As of this moment there are no survivors. On behalf of Pan-Con — "

I hung up.

"Who was that?" Lori said, taking a carrot from the refrigerator.

"Nobody." I walked into the living room, stumbled over the couch pillows on the floor, threw them across the room. "Get the vacuum!" I yelled at Lori. "They're going to be home any minute. Let's clean up this pigpen." I pushed a chair across the room, knocked over a lamp.

"Hey! What happened?" Lori said, getting in my way. "Why are you so mad? Who was that on the phone?"

I turned on lights, the TV, turned up the sound. "That stupid woman!"

"What woman? Will you tell me what's going on?" Lori shouted.

"On the phone . . . she's crazy. She called me before and asked for somebody named Bo."

"The same woman?"

"Yes! No! How should I know?" She hadn't sounded crazy at all. She talked like somebody in an office carefully reading a message she'd been handed. Like the announcements in school over the PA system. The person just read what was handed her. She didn't know if the message was true or not. She had kept asking me was this where the Kellers lived. *Phil Keller.* . . . She didn't even have our names right. What crash was she talking about? If there had been

10

a real crash there would have been survivors. There were always survivors.

"What are you crying for?"

"I'm not crying. Will you do some work instead of staring at me."

"Billy, what happened?"

"They said Mom and Dad's plane crashed."

She stood with her mouth open, flecks of carrot on her tongue. I couldn't bear her face. "It was a mistake! I told you it was a mistake!"

She followed me into the kitchen. I pushed the dishes into the sink. I couldn't find the plug or the detergent. I held a broken dish in my hands. "Mom's going to be really mad when she sees this."

"But that woman said — "

"What does she know? It was just a phone call. Anybody can call up and say anything they want."

"Maybe Kevin can find out." Lori was shaking.

"Kevin's in college. He's not here." There was a clamoring in my head. "Wash the dishes. Are you going to help me or not?"

She ran from the room. I let the sink fill up with suds. "Billy — " she called a moment later. "Billy," she screamed. "Billy, come here, quick!"

On the TV, the news announcer was reading a special bulletin. He had a square face, like a bulldog, with horn-rimmed glasses. "I repeat this special bulletin. Late this afternoon a Pan-Con charter flight exploded in midair over the Caribbean with eighty-seven passengers and crew members on board. A bomb is suspected. Rescue ships and helicopters are

11

rushing to the area, but as of this moment there are no reports of survivors."

Lori clung to my arm, digging her fingers into me. The announcer disappeared. Now a boy and a girl were sitting at a table eating. Behind them their mother was smiling. I watched them dumbly. I felt nothing.

Chapter 3

I watched the morning light edge into the window of my room, then slide silently along the wall. It lit up my favorite poster, autumn maples blazing with golden light. At home in Delmar there were two trees exactly like that across the road from our house. One year my mother photographed those trees every couple of weeks from before they blossomed in the spring till the leaves fell in the autumn. I'd look out of my window and see her standing in the road below the maples, eye to the viewfinder. A truck couldn't move her when she was concentrating. Those pictures won her a prize in a Kodak contest.

Mom loved morning light. She and my father both were a couple of early birds. In the morning I'd lie in bed and hear them talking in their room, the bathroom, or the kitchen. The radio would be on, and I'd hear the drone of news and weather as the smell of perking coffee filled the house.

I lay on the bed, hands stretched above me intersecting the light, Mom's light, listening for their voices.

Begin again. A nursery rhyme my mother sang was in my head. *There was an old woman who swallowed a fly. I don't know why she swallowed the fly. I think she'll die. . . . Begin again. . . . There was an old woman who swallowed a spider who squirmed and squiggled and wiggled inside her. I don't know why . . . I think she'll die.*

I wanted to be little again and say I was sorry and I'd never do it again, and then they'd come home.

I lay there a long time, focusing my thoughts on the bus from Boston that was bringing my brother home.

Last night it had taken us a long time to get Kevin on the phone. His roommate said he was studying. I called back five minutes later. Kevin still wasn't there. I called again. "Look, he's in the library. . . ."

Later when Kevin called, Lori and I were watching the TV, waiting for the eleven o'clock news. The phone rang. It scared me, and then I thought it was good news, and I got twice as scared.

"What happened?" Kevin said.

I couldn't talk. I stumbled . . . stuttered. I couldn't get the words out straight. Lori finally told him.

All that first day people kept coming to the house — neighborhood people — ringing the bell

14

and asking if we were the ones. The story about the crash was in the newspaper and on the TV. A woman who lived across the street said she heard it on *The Morning Show.* She was wearing a blue bathrobe and her hair was in curlers. "You poor kids, both your parents. . . ."

My nose ached high in the bridge. I mumbled, "Thanks," then ducked back inside. Lori was smarter. She never answered the door.

Mrs. Stein came downstairs and stayed with us all day. She kept making us things to eat. Steve and Holly, who lived in the basement apartment, came up, too. Steve, who was a reporter for TV, didn't have anything to say. Holly was the talker. I was glad she was there. She kept things going. She even told us some jokes. Lori started laughing and couldn't stop.

When our schools called, Holly talked to them. "Billy?" She put her hand over the phone. "Your principal wants to know who's here with you kids."

"You're here and Mrs. Stein — "

She rolled her eyes. "I know I'm here, but who's the mature, responsible adult?"

"My brother's coming home from Boston."

All day I waited for Kevin. Every time the doorbell or the phone rang I thought it was him, and then he came home and it was nothing. He walked in carrying a knapsack and dragging a heavy suitcase across the floor. I hadn't seen him since before we moved. He handed me the knapsack. "Hang it in the closet." His first words to me.

He looked different. He'd cut his hair short, and

the gold-rimmed glasses were new. He looked older, but what I really thought was, he didn't look old enough. For a while he sniffed around like a cat in a strange house. "What's there to eat?" he said. Lori hung on him, and I followed wherever he went.

"What are we going to do?" I said. I'd been waiting for him. I wanted him to get things going, tell me what was going to happen. I wanted to get rid of this hard, scared feeling inside me.

"Later," he said. "We'll talk later. Okay?"

But later, he took out his books and studied. Lori and I watched TV and ate frozen chocolate cake.

Lori was falling asleep against my shoulder when the phone rang. She came awake hard. "Who is it? Daddy's on the phone?"

Kevin got the phone in the hall. "Yes, we're all right, Uncle John."

Uncle John was Dad's younger brother. There were just the two of them, Uncle John and my father. Uncle John was a pipe welder and mechanic, and went all over the world to work. He'd sent us a box of dates from Egypt and a saddle blanket from Lebanon, and we were always getting crates of oranges from California. Once he'd sent me a blue polka-dot cap like the ones welders wore. But we weren't close to him the way we were to Aunt Joan and to Uncle Paul, who was Mom's brother.

Lori wrapped her arms around herself. "Billy, I thought it was Daddy."

"It isn't."

"It could be. Why not? They could have fallen into the water and been picked up by a fishing boat, or swum to an island. You know how good Mom and Dad can swim."

"You don't really believe that, do you?"

"Yes, I do."

"Oh, Lori. . . ."

When Kevin got off the phone he came and sat with us on the floor. He yawned and slumped. "I told Uncle John that Uncle Paul and Aunt Joan are coming tomorrow so he said he'd wait in case we needed him later." Kevin rubbed his cheek. "He sounds just like Dad on the phone. He was crying." Kevin's eyes filled and he took his glasses off.

"They are alive," Lori said. "I know they're alive. They have to be." She threw herself against Kevin and he held her.

"Lori, honey, nobody on that plane is alive. The plane blew up in the air. There are just too many facts. Nothing's been found, not even one body. Nothing but a few lousy pieces of wreckage."

I took a walk down the hall and back to the living room and down the hall again. Every time I went by their room I looked. The bed was untouched, the yellow sheet neatly turned over the quilt. Everything the way Mom had left it — the window open a crack, the long, loose legs of my father's pajamas stirring on the hanger.

When I was little I used to get into bed with them in the morning, climb in between them. Sometimes my father would put his knees up and I'd climb up Father Mountain and then down to Mother Mountain.

The next morning I was the first one up. I opened

17

Lori's door a crack. I hardly made a sound but she rolled over instantly, her eyes wide open, as if she'd been lying awake for hours.

"They're alive, Billy!" Her face was wrinkled and red with sleep. "They're safe on an island."

"Get up," I said. "Get dressed and we'll have breakfast."

"I can't eat. My stomach hurts too much."

"It was that cake."

"Don't talk to me." She thrashed around, kicked her covers. "Everything hurts . . . everything."

I leaned against her bed, suddenly tired. "You're not going to stay in bed all day, are you?"

Kevin was asleep on the living-room couch, his head covered. Light streamed in through the plants in front of the windows. I sat down on the floor and waited for him to wake up. There was a time when I could have been my brother's dog and been happy. I used to follow him everywhere. I even walked pigeon-toed the way he did.

Once when I was six or seven, I followed Kevin and his friends into the woods behind our house in Delmar and hid behind a tree. They made a fire, fried kielbasi on sticks, and roasted potatoes. I ran up and sat next to my brother. "Hi." He pushed me away. So I put my foot in the fire to make his friends laugh.

"I smell rubber burning," someone said.

I kept smiling.

"Does it hurt yet?"

"Uh, uh."

Kevin yanked me away, hit me, then pulled my sneaker off and packed wet leaves around my foot.

He was afraid I'd go home crying, and he'd be blamed. But I wasn't crying. I was laughing. My brother was taking care of me and feeding me greasy chunks of kielbasi and the best part of a potato he poked from the ashes.

On the couch Kevin stirred, turned, and opened his eyes.

"What are you doing?"

"Guarding you." I stretched out on the floor, hands behind my head, admiring my brother. Even sitting up, half asleep, he looked impressive — long and blond with a long smooth torso. I was more like Dad with my hairy arms and legs. King Kong Keller and Kevin the Viking.

"You could use a little hair on your chest, brother. I hear that women like fuzzy men. Doesn't Kathy complain?"

"She hasn't yet." Kevin rubbed his eyes, then reached under the couch for his glasses. The thin gold rims made him look like a doctor already.

"How long have you had them?"

"What?"

"Those glasses?"

"I've worn them since tenth grade."

"I never knew that."

"Shows how observant you are. What else don't you remember about me?"

"The elephant never forgets. How about those great fights we used to have?"

"What fights? You'd come after me and I'd flatten you."

Kevin pulled on his jeans. "Let's go, Billy. Uncle

19

Paul and Aunt Joan are coming today. Maybe Grandma Betty, too. We've got to clean up."

I got up on my knees. "Let's see if you can still take me."

"Come on, Billy, stop playing. We've got things to do." He stuck his feet into his sneakers. There it was — put down like a dumb kid, and like a kid I got stubborn and stayed there on the floor. Much good it did me. Kevin walked out and left me there.

Kevin took charge. He tied a red bandana around his forehead. "Eggs for breakfast."

"I'm not hungry," Lori said.

"I want you to eat."

"I'm never going to eat again." She sat on the windowsill, holding her guitar against her cheek.

"Come on, honey. Everything's going to be all right. I'm home now." He popped the bread into the toaster.

That's the way you ought to talk, Kevin. It was what I'd been waiting for him to say. Yesterday he'd been like a visitor. Today he was the way he should be, taking charge.

He kept us moving, made us clean up after we ate, then told me to get out the vacuum and do the halls and the living room. "Lori and I are going to clean the bathrooms. You two have been living here like a couple of slobs."

When I got lazy, he muscled me around. I needed to be pushed. He tied a red bandana around Lori's forehead like the one he was wearing. "Come on, lamby." He kept calling her honey and lamby. It made me a little jealous. I was the one who lived with Lori. Kevin had hardly been around these last few years since he went to college.

With the three of us working we got the house straightened up and we still had time. Too much time. We started passing Lori's basketball around in the living room, then we went outside and down the street to the playground. Cars roared down Dyer Avenue. I looked up at the blue sky and saw the plane split apart into a thousand pieces.

It was a clear, cold day and there was nobody at the playground except a couple of bundled-up little kids and their mothers. "It feels funny being here on a school day," Lori said.

We had the basketball court to ourselves. It was two on one, Lori and the Apeman against Kevin the Viking. I kept driving against Kevin. I wanted to get the ball past him, but I couldn't score till I passed to Lori and she dropped the ball in. "Three times," she yelled and held three fingers up in Kevin's face. "Three times we beat you."

Going back to the house we fooled around, passing the basketball back and forth, arguing and yelling at each other. Uncle Paul and Aunt Joan were waiting for us in front of the house. It was so unreal that for a second I thought they were dressed up cardboard cutouts somebody had set in front of the house. Grandma Betty was sitting on the steps, leaning her head against the railing.

"Grandma!" Lori ran up to her. Kevin shook hands with Uncle Paul and embraced Aunt Joan. Just then

21

the ball popped out of my arm and I ran into the street after it. "Billy!" Aunt Joan cried. "Be careful."

I stood in the street, ashamed because I was holding the basketball, ashamed because I had been playing and had forgotten everything.

Chapter 4

We all went inside and sat around the living room. It was awkward. Grandma Betty sat with her arm around Lori. Aunt Joan and Uncle Paul were so glum. They were just sitting there. Did they think they had to act that way because of us? Were they afraid to smile? *Cheer up. If Mom and Dad walked in right now they wouldn't like to see you this way.* Mom never liked to sit around. She'd get things moving.

Dad would have his joke, too. *There's been a slight mistake,* he'd say. *We were never on that plane to begin with.* Then he'd give me a wink. *I hope you're all not too disappointed.*

"Billy!" Aunt Joan said. "What are you doing?"

"Me?" I looked down at my lap — dust, a broken

crayon, bits of paper. I'd been pulling things out from under the couch pillows.

"You're all so big," Uncle Paul said, and he shook his head like it was a miracle we'd grown up at all. "How's college, Kevin? Keeping your marks up?"

Grandma Betty sighed. "Are you children hungry?"

"Mom, not now." Uncle Paul pulled at his tie. He had my mother's wiry blond hair. Even the red around his eyes was like hers when she was upset.

Later, while Grandma Betty lay down to rest, Aunt Joan went out shopping with Lori. Kevin drove. "Well!" Uncle Paul rubbed his hands together. "Here we are." He put his arm around my shoulders. "You and I are going to go over the house together. Everything in detail," he said, "starting with the top floor."

"There's nothing to see up there, Uncle Paul. Dad and I were working on the apartment."

"I want to see what you got done," he said.

Upstairs, I had to move the Sheetrock out of the way so I could open the door.

"So you helped your dad do all this?" Uncle Paul said, looking around.

"Sure," I said, remembering all the times Dad had to keep after me to do anything.

The skylight was the best thing about the top floor apartment. You could climb out on the roof and look out over all the buildings. "I don't like skylights," Uncle Paul said. "They leak, and anybody can break in just by smashing the glass. A lot of work still to be done up here," he added.

24

"Dad didn't have much time," I said and I started crying.

Uncle Paul waited for me to stop. He didn't make a fuss. He didn't comment. I liked him for that.

Mrs. Stein didn't want to let us into her apartment at first. She thought Uncle Paul was here to buy the house and make them move.

"I'm Billy's uncle from Flint, Michigan. I just want to look around."

She held me back. "Your mother and father didn't put old people out on the street."

"We're not selling the house, Mrs. Stein," I said, but I was embarrassed because I didn't know what Uncle Paul had in mind.

Steve and Holly weren't home downstairs. Uncle Paul peered through the windows. "I see what it is. Let's see the rest of the house."

I showed him the cellar, the big boiler, and the oil furnace that heated the whole house.

"Oil is dirty," Uncle Paul said. "I like gas better. The walls are cracking."

"We're going to put a waterproof cement over it."

Outside, he squinted at the roof. "Those eaves don't look so hot."

"It's a good roof," I said defensively. Uncle Paul talked as if my father didn't know anything. Dad had seen these things, too. "We were going to do everything," I said. "It takes time." (My father's words.) "We've only lived here a few months."

"Who's going to do it now? A contractor wants his weight in gold just to come into the house."

"I can do the work."

Uncle Paul acted like he didn't hear me. "What rents are you collecting?"

I showed him the receipt book Mom kept on her work table. He sat down with it, put on his glasses, and went over everything. "The downstairs rent's okay but the upstairs apartment isn't getting half of what it should."

"Dad didn't want to raise their rent."

"The bills still have to be paid."

"The Steins are old."

"I'm not saying your father was wrong. More people ought to be like him. We can't all be hard-headed businessmen, right?" He gave me a bright, knowing look. Mom's eyes, but they weren't at all alike.

That night we all ate together in the dining room — white tablecloth, place settings. Not like us. Not like our family. There was a platter of roast beef and mashed potatoes. Aunt Joan asked us to dress for dinner. Lori had to take off her sweat shirt and put on a white blouse, and I changed my jeans.

I was hungry. Aunt Joan filled up my plate. I couldn't wait to start eating and then I remembered and lost my appetite. I was ashamed to be eating.

"Pass the bread, please . . . and the butter. Did you take enough meat?" Aunt Joan said. "Take more, Billy. Lori, you're not eating anything." She kept wanting to refill our plates. "Billy, you're not eating, either. Aren't you hungry?"

"Him not hungry?" Uncle Paul said. "When did you see a kid who wasn't hungry?

26

"Good meat," Uncle Paul said. There was a dark stain of gravy next to his plate.

"I had to call the butcher to get the cut I wanted," Aunt Joan said.

"It's very juicy," Uncle Paul said. "Ma, you're not eating anything. You haven't eaten that little slice I gave you."

I mashed the peas slowly into the potatoes. I was remembering our cat Petty in Delmar, the way she used to sit in my lap at the table and I'd feed her scraps. No matter how much we fed her she still brought home birds, mice, chipmunks. Once she brought home a baby rabbit, still alive, with its guts hanging out. Dad drowned it in a pail of water.

"Are you through, Billy?" Aunt Joan said. "You're not going to leave all that good food, are you? Lori, you're eating nicely, but there's too much butter on your plate. You shouldn't eat so much butter. That's what puts pounds on you."

Lori dropped her knife and sat staring at her plate. She was sensitive about her weight. "Just take a little butter at a time," Aunt Joan said soothingly.

"None of us needs all that fat," Uncle Paul said. "Am I right, Kevin? You're our medical expert. Butter's nothing but fat, Lori."

Lori jumped up.

"Hey, Lori," Kevin said softly. "Sit down."

"If you're leaving the table, Lori," Aunt Joan said, "you should excuse yourself. Your mother, I know, taught you manners."

"Yes, she did." Lori's eyes were shut tight. "She taught us thoughtfulness and consideration for other

27

people's feelings." She ran from the room.

"Young lady!" Uncle Paul said.

"Not now," Aunt Joan said. "Let her go, Paul." They exchanged a look. "I shouldn't have said anything."

Later my aunt called me into the kitchen to help with the dishes. I washed and she dried and put things away. Occasionally she'd ask where something went. "Tomato juice?"

"Refrigerator door."

"Bread?"

"Box in that cupboard."

"Thank you, Billy." She sighed. "I'm worried about your cousins. I left them with a responsible woman, but my boys are lost without me. I can't stop thinking if it had been us — you children are so brave — my boys would have fallen apart by now."

I let my hands slide into the warm soapy water, let them go limp and sink down to the bottom, drowned them. Why hadn't I fallen apart? What was wrong with me?

In my room, Lori was lying on my bed reading a comic book. "They're going to sleep in Mom and Dad's room," she said. "Kevin said it was all right."

"Move over." I lay down on the bed and pulled the pillow over my head.

"What's that matter with you?" Lori said.

"Nothing. I don't feel like talking."

A little later Kevin came in and tossed his sleeping bag in the corner. "I'm sleeping in here tonight, Billy."

"Shut the door," Lori said. "Why are they staying in Mom and Dad's room?"

"Where are they supposed to stay?" Kevin said. "Grandma Betty's going to sleep in the living room."

"They can afford a motel," Lori said. "They're so tight and stingy. Did you see what mean little eyes Aunt Joan has?"

"Come on, Lori." Kevin lay down at the foot of the bed. "Give the lady a break, honey. Being here is a strain on them, too."

"The only one I like is Grandma Betty. She's nice, and I'll tell you something, they don't like us, either. Isn't that right, Billy?"

I shrugged.

"They're not the most sensitive people in the world," Kevin said. "The important thing is they're here, they're family, they care." He polished his glasses on the sheet. "Uncle Paul wants me to talk to you kids about something." He put his glasses on again. "He wants to have a funeral for Mom and Dad."

I sat up. "No funeral. You need bodies for a funeral and we don't . . . you know . . . oh, forget it." I fell back down and pulled the pillow over my face.

"We have to do something, some kind of service," Kevin said. "That's what people do. Kathy's family had a home service when her grandfather died. Just the family and a few friends. They talked about her grandfather and then they had a quiet time to think about him. Uncle Paul should go for that."

"Uncle Paul, Uncle Paul," Lori said. "What makes him so important all of a sudden?"

29

Kevin patted her knee. "Take it easy, fireball. What do you want to do, Billy?"

"The service sounds all right." Lori gave me a dirty look. "Kevin's right," I said. "We've got to do something."

She reached for the comic book. "Do whatever you want," she said.

Later in bed I heard my aunt and uncle in Mom and Dad's room. As soon as this was over they'd be going back to their own kids. And then — what about us? We'd be alone. I hadn't let myself really think about it before. Once they were gone, Kevin would go back to college and Lori and I would be alone again. How were we going to live? Was Uncle Paul going to help us? Were they that rich? Could they pay for this house and their house, too? Was he going to tell us to raise the rents so we'd have more money? I lay there not knowing . . . and then I knew.

Nobody was going to let a sixteen-year-old and a twelve-year-old live alone. That was why Uncle Paul had gone over every inch and detail of the house so carefully. The house was going to be sold and we were going to live with them.

I didn't want to go. I didn't want to leave this house. I didn't want anything to change. I didn't want what was left of our family broken up. I wanted us to live together, not just Lori and me. Lori, Kevin, and me, the three of us together. That's what I wanted. That's all I wanted.

We could stay if Kevin stayed. It was that simple and it was that impossible.

Chapter 5

For the week that Aunt Joan and Uncle Paul were with us, I got up late every morning, stayed in bed a lot. Was I grieving? I felt empty, with no desire to do anything. How could it have happened? I thought about it every day but I never got closer to understanding. Who had done this to me? Why? Why me? Why us?

There was that moment of waking when I almost believed Mom and Dad were in the other room, getting dressed, or making breakfast, waiting for us to get up. That crazy surge of hope, the adrenaline racing like a fire through my veins! Then I'd hear the voices of my aunt and uncle and I'd wrap my arms around my belly, around that pain in my gut. I wanted to be little again, to curl up and grow smaller and smaller . . . till I was so small I could fall through the cracks in the floor. . . .

"Billy!" *My father was yelling from the driveway.* "If *you want a ride to school get a move on. I haven't got all day.*"

"Wait, Dad, don't go without me." *The sun shone and the whippy, snake-sided tree banged against the house.*

Sometimes the talk at dinner got around to the future. Just hints of things about how good it would be for Lori and me to get away from here, go someplace fresh. I tuned out. In the back of my mind, buried deep, there was still hope. I hardly admitted it to myself. I knew the facts. There was no hope . . . but still every day, there was the story of how they would come home, the same story, on and on in my head.

The morning of the memorial service I was in bed long after everyone else was up. I heard Kevin talking to my aunt and then someone started vacuuming. Grandma Betty came in to see how I was doing. "Hey, sleepy head, how long are you going to stay in bed?" She picked my jeans up from the floor. The makeup and powder she wore only made her look more tired.

"You don't have to do that, Grandma."

"Do you mind? I'm sorry. But this room looks like the three little piggies live here."

"Not piggies, Grandma. Just one big slob."

"Tell me the difference."

"Pigs are pigs," I said, "but slobs know the difference."

She sat down next to me and smoothed my hair. "Your hair is like hers, not the color, but it feels just the same." She started to cry.

"Grandma. . . ."

"I'm sorry," she said. "I shouldn't cry in front of the children. . . . I know I'm making you feel bad." She knelt down and rolled up Kevin's sleeping bag.

Later I put on a white shirt and a pair of painter's pants.

I went out. Lori was polishing the furniture in the living room. She was wearing a yellow embroidered blouse over her jeans, and her hair was combed out, shining and ripply as water.

"You look like a garbage man," she said. "You're not supposed to wear white."

"The Chinese wear white when they mourn."

"Why?"

"Maybe they know something we don't. "

Aunt Joan had placed Mom and Dad's wedding picture on a table, unlit candles on either side, a bowl of yellow roses in back. In the picture Mom's hair was pulled back tight with a ribbon, and she wore a little hat, like a crown. She and Dad were holding hands. I lit the candles, then Lori got her incense and put it on the table.

I sat with Grandma for a while. Then I went to get her some tea. In the kitchen, platters of food covered with silver paper were lined up as if an army were coming.

"Don't touch," Aunt Joan said. "I was up late doing this."

I brought Grandma her tea, then wandered around,

my hands clasped behind me like a skater, looking this way and that, not stopping any place for long. A smile, a nod, a polite phrase. Skating, on the surface, on top of things, smooth as ice. "How are you doing, Uncle Paul? Did you sleep well last night?" I really wanted them all to go, to leave us so we could be by ourselves, Lori and me, and Kevin, too.

The Steins were the first to come. Mrs. Stein brought more food in a covered dish and handed it to Aunt Joan in that crooked way she had. Mr. Stein accepted a jigger of Old Crow from Uncle Paul. "This much." Mr. Stein held up three fingers. "No ice, and no ginger ale, either. I like it neat."

"Say hello to Mr. and Mrs. Stein," Aunt Joan said, as if they'd come from afar. I skated over, bobbed, and bowed. "Greetings," I said and skated on.

When Steve and Holly came up I offered them a drink. "Ginger ale for me," Steve said, "in case I have to drive."

"I'm getting pregnant," Holly whispered. "I'll have orange soda."

Why so quiet, Holly? It's not like you. And why was everyone talking in such low voices? Who were they afraid of waking? "See you," I said in my normal, loud voice and skated off to get their drinks.

In the kitchen I poured myself three fingers' worth like Mr. Stein and took it down neat. My throat burned and then my stomach lit up. I wiped my eyes, then put in a little more whiskey and a lot of ice and ginger ale.

I skated around. Everyone was buzzing; they were

like insects going round and round in my head. Steve was telling Uncle Paul and Mr. Stein about his job with station WKTV and the things that happened when he did street interviews. Holly sat near Kevin, who wore a soft gray turtleneck shirt. Lori was plunking on her guitar. I sat down next to Grandma again and we moved our heads in time to the music.

So this was what a home service was, this quiet party. Was this what Kevin had meant? Were we all thinking about Mom and Dad now? I grabbed Kevin's arm when he came by. "I think we ought to start, Kevin, my man."

A few more neighbors came in from our street, but it was mainly our family and the people who lived in the house. Uncle Paul loosened his tie. "I want to thank you all for coming."

"Thank people for coming to a funeral, or a home service . . . or whatever you call it."

"Shh!" Kevin poked me.

"This is a very sad occasion," Uncle Paul said and then he stopped like he'd forgotten what he wanted to say.

"Come on, come on, talk." I wanted him to talk, say what he was going to say and get it over with. "Go," I said. "Go, man, go." Kevin clamped his hand over my mouth. I slumped down in my chair.

"Who would have dreamed this could have happened?" Uncle Paul said. "To come to the end like that, taken out of life, right at their prime, when they had everything to live for. It makes you wonder what life's all about. They had such dreams for their kids." He put his hand on Kevin's knee. "My nephew

35

here is going to be a fine doctor some day. My sister and her husband had their hearts set on that. They wanted their children to get someplace in the world and I promise you it's going to happen."

His voice filled. "Good hard-working people, they worked their tails off for their kids." He shook his head. "I can think of a lot of people I'd rather see dead."

"Come on, honey," Aunt Joan said, "don't talk that way."

Next, Mr. Stein spoke. "The Lord giveth and He taketh away." He had to stop and catch his breath because of the emphysema. "The ways of the Lord are beyond our knowing."

"Amen," Mrs. Stein said. "I pray for these poor children."

Lori picked at her guitar, her head bent so you couldn't see her face, and played Mom's favorite Beatles tunes. I'm next, I thought, and panicked because my mind was a mess.

But then Kevin spoke. "Our parents," he said and squeezed my shoulder hard. "We took them for granted. They were here. We thought they'd always be here." His fingers were digging into my shoulder. *Don't say something stupid, Kevin.* "As Uncle Paul said, they were good parents. They were good, they were very good, they were the best parents. We loved them, we love them still, we'll always love and honor them."

Lori stopped playing. I looked up at the ceiling. No tears, please . . . this is a white funeral, not a black one. On the table I saw Kevin's cracked graduation picture. There was a fullness in my nose, a pain high in the bridge of my nose . . . in my head . . . my throat . . . something wild calling out. . . .

Ma . . . Ma. . . . It was nighttime in Delmar, and I was in my Dr. Denton's standing by the window bellowing for my mother at the top of my lungs. They weren't home. . . . Ma . . . Ma . . . Ma. . . .

I stood up. Don't look, don't anyone look. I rushed out.

Upstairs in the unfinished apartment everything lay open and exposed. My father's two-foot square hung on a nail and beneath it the flat wooden toolbox that had belonged to my father's father, who was a carpenter and had passed his tools on to his son. I opened the box, took out a hammer, the four chisels in their canvas case. My father liked good tools, sharp-edged with strong wooden handles and solid brass heads.

I squatted there for a while, then put on my father's denim work apron and walked slowly around the room, crying and hitting the woodwork with a hammer. *Drunk, you're stupid, dizzy drunk.* That's all I could think. *You got drunk at your parents' funeral.*

Chapter 6

In the dining room, Aunt Joan was wrapping glasses in newspaper. All our good glassware, bowls, and pitchers were out on the table. There were boxes on the floor, Mom's shoes were lined up along the wall. Grandma Betty was in the kitchen, emptying the cupboards, sorting and stacking dishes. Yesterday the service. Today they were packing up. Packing us up. Getting us ready to move, but still nobody had said anything officially.

"How are you this morning, Billy?" Aunt Joan smiled. "I don't think you combed your hair. You boys. You're just like Ross in the morning. It takes him forever to get ready for school."

"What's going on, Aunt Joan? Why's everyone so busy?"

She stuffed newspapers into a row of glasses. "This is such a lovely bowl," she said, holding up a cut-glass bowl. The light through the glass made rainbows dance on the wall. "Didn't that come from your great-aunt Louise?"

"Aunt Joan, why are you packing everything up?"

"Careful, Billy." Aunt Joan moved some glasses. "We're going to talk about everything this morning, just as soon as the men get back from the bakery. It will just be a little longer. So please be patient."

The men. . . . What was I, a baby? Why couldn't they just give us the medicine and get it over with. They made a production of everything. Our family wasn't like that. We never dressed up to eat. We didn't have a formal living room or a lot of fancy furniture. We were like the old, saggy brown couch in the living room that had been with us for as long as I could remember.

Lori sat cross-legged on the floor, arranging pieces on the checkerboard. Did she want to go with them? Would she stay here if I did? Why hadn't we talked about these things? I blamed myself. I blamed Kevin. He was going back to school, but Lori and I were the ones whose lives were going to change.

If Kevin stays, we can stay. The same impossible idea again. *If Kevin stays, we can stay.* Was it so impossible? There were schools here for him. He wouldn't have to take care of us, just be here. Lori and I would take care of the house, we'd cook, clean up the mess. We knew how to do that already. If Kevin stayed it would be better for everyone, not just us. Uncle Paul and Aunt Joan wouldn't have to think about us or worry about selling the house and getting rid of the furniture. They could go home and take care of their own family.

"When's Kevin coming back?" I said to Lori. "I've got to talk to him." I knelt down and moved a checker. *If Kevin stays, we can stay.* I jumped up and looked out the window. What was taking them so long?

"Are you playing or not?" Lori said.

"Where'd you move?"

"Do I have to move for you, too?"

I picked up a checker. "I . . . move . . . here."

Lori leaned over the board. "And I jump you here. That's what happens when you don't pay attention."

"What are we going to do with all these shoes?" Aunt Joan called. Mom had more shoes than the rest of the family combined. Most of the time she wore the same worn-down pair of Bass moccasins, but she couldn't resist a pretty pair of shoes on sale.

"I want them," Lori said.

"All of them?" Aunt Joan said.

"Yes!"

Aunt Joan sighed. "I'll just put them in boxes, then, and label them. That way we'll know where they are."

"Lori." I leaned over the board. "Do you know what they're doing?"

"Billy, I'm going to sleep if you don't make a move fast."

"Forget checkers, Lori. They're moving us out of here. We're going to be living with them, with Aunt Joan and Uncle Paul."

"I know."

"I'll probably share a room with Ross."

"That conceited ass. Don't make me sick!"

"Would you like to stay here, in our own house?"

She looked furiously down at the board. "We go where we're told or they'll put a leash on us and take us anyway. I quit. This game is stupid. I suppose you can't wait to go live with them!"

"You suppose wrong."

Lori grabbed my hand and whispered, "Let's run away, Billy. I've got money saved. How much have you got?"

I moved over next to her. "Now listen to me, Lori. If Kevin stayed, we could, too."

"Kevin? What does that mean?"

"He can go to college here. It makes sense. He's the head of the family now. Twenty-one is legal, Lori. All he has to do is tell them the three of us are going to live together, here, in our own house." Yes, I thought, our own house, where Mom and Dad would want us to be.

When Kevin came in I grabbed him at the door. "Kevin!" I got up close to him. "I want you to stay."

"What?"

"I've figured it out. If you stay we can stay. Go to school here, get your degree — "

"Slow down, Billy. Everything's worked out."

I grabbed his arm. "Nothing's worked out. I don't want to go, and Lori doesn't either. . . ."

"Billy." Uncle Paul pulled me aside. He had Sunday's newspaper folded to an inside page. "They did a story on the crash. Do you want to see it? You don't

41

have to." Then he handed it to me.

It was a feature story about the plane crash with photos of the plane and the pilots and hostesses. My eyes jumped to the passenger list. *Joseph Keller* and then *Phil Keller* beneath it. They still had Mom's name spelled wrong.

"Kevin," I yelled. He'd walked out on me.

Aunt Joan handed me a tray with sweet rolls and butter. "Quiet down, quiet down. We're all going in the living room now where we can sit and talk comfortably."

I saw a signal pass between Uncle Paul and Aunt Joan. "Sit down, everyone. Billy, you, too." He caught my eye and winked as if we understood each other perfectly.

Aunt Joan passed the sweet rolls around. "Billy?" I shook my head. I was too nervous to eat.

Uncle Paul buttered a roll. "I know how hard everything's been on you kids — and maybe I'm rushing things, but I think we'd better get to it. We have business we've got to discuss." He loosened his collar. "Let's talk about money. You've got a little in the bank, plus you'll be getting social security and some life insurance. Plus there may be a settlement with the airline's insurance company. But that's a long way down the pike. The house won't bring much. Too big a mortgage and the real-estate agent will take the rest. I just hope we can break even on that. We should be able to take care of the rest of Kevin's college education and get him started in medical school."

"The children don't have to know all these money

42

details," Aunt Joan said. She smoothed Lori's hair. "Your parents aren't going to rest till they know you children are being taken care of. We're not going to let you down. We feel about you the same as we do about our own boys."

I swung around. Kevin was leaning against the wall behind me. Now was the time for him to say something. *Thanks, Uncle Paul and Aunt Joan. We really appreciate everything you're doing but we've got our own plans.*

"This whole thing comes at a bad time for us," Uncle Paul said. "I've got a machine tool convention coming up next week, and Aunt Joan is over her head in our tax work and government forms." He put down his cup. "The point is, we can't settle everything in one shot. We're going to have to go home and come back. It's a mess but we'll manage."

Why didn't Kevin speak? No mess if we did things right.

"We'll do this in stages," Uncle Paul continued. "Stage one is getting you kids settled in your new school. Then we can start thinking about unloading the house."

"You don't have to — " I started.

"Billy, please," Aunt Joan said. "You're interrupting your Uncle Paul. It's your future he's talking about."

"Billy, you'll come live with us," Uncle Paul said. "You'll room with your cousin Ross. It's going to be a little tight but I think the two of you can manage. Lori will live with Grandma Betty."

"Not with Billy?" Lori said.

Grandma Betty leaned forward and patted her back. "You're going to be my own little girl now."

I stood up next to Kevin. "Did you hear what they just said? They're going to split us up. Is that what you want?"

"We're going to fix up your room together, Lori," Grandma Betty went on. "You can pick out your own material, whatever colors you decide. Isn't that lovely? My eyes aren't so good, so you'll thread the machine for me and I'll sew the curtains."

"Ma," Uncle Paul said. "Not now."

"Don't look so upset, Billy," Aunt Joan said. "It's going to work out fine. I like boys. I have two of my own. You're going to like living with us."

Like . . . like . . . where did they get the idea that Lori and I would *like* being separated? We were brother and sister. We had lived together all our lives.

"Kevin and I had a long talk this morning," Uncle Paul said, "and he's agreed to stay with you two this week and maybe next week, too, till we can get back."

Aunt Joan leaned forward. "We'll be back to get you, I promise."

"You've got it wrong, Uncle Paul," I said. "You don't have to come back. You don't have to sell the house. You don't have to worry about us. If Kevin stays home, we can stay together in this house. Mom and Dad aren't here, but we can take care of ourselves. That's what we should be talking about."

Uncle Paul was smiling. "Don't get so excited, Billy. I know you'd like to help but that would never

44

work. Let Aunt Joan and me figure things out."

I turned to Kevin. I'd said it, but now he had to say it. "Kevin! Don't stand there holding up the wall. Tell them you're going to stay. Talk, Kevin!"

My brother was looking off into space. Smiling. But that smile — it was no smile at all. His teeth were clenched. The smile was congealed on his face — a smear of grease — and I finally realized that Kevin wasn't going to stay, didn't want to stay. My brother didn't care if we were separated, didn't care what happened to us so long as he got what he wanted.

And then the anger welled up in me, rose up to my throat, spilled out like poison. "Damn you, Kevin, I hope you die."

"Billy, what's happening to you?" Aunt Joan said.

"What's going on, boys?" Uncle Paul said.

I turned away. My eyes filled. My stupid eyes. "Crud!" I whispered and ran out of the house.

Kevin came running out after me. "Hold it, you jerk."

I shook him off. "You pig. You're letting them split us up. Lori one place. Me another. We're not even a family anymore."

Kevin grabbed my arm. "Come on! Let's talk, Billy."

I looked back. Aunt Joan was watching from the window. "Not here."

We got into the Mercedes. "Drive someplace," I said.

Chapter 7

I sat with my back to the car door, staring at my brother. What a good-looking, honest guy he appeared to be with his straight nose and forthright chin. They could have stamped his face on a coin. Mr. Charm. He could sing and make everything sound beautiful. *Listen, you two, I'm home now. There's nothing to worry about.* The hypocrite.

Didn't he know I was scared? Wasn't he scared? Mom and Dad were gone. We were alone and I was scared. At night I didn't sleep. I was afraid to close my eyes. If we broke up, there would be nothing left. No more Kellers.

Kevin turned down South Avenue the wrong way. A red Mustang screeched on its brakes. "You moron," the Mustang driver yelled. "Don't you read signs?"

"Why don't *you* look where you're driving!" I yelled back.

Kevin swung around and almost ran into another car. "Crappy driver. . . ." He jammed the brakes and parked the car a mile from the curb. "I have to have something to drink." He ran into a luncheonette. I followed him. I wasn't letting him out of my sight.

"A large orange juice," he ordered. "You want something?" he said over his shoulder. I shook my head. "I can't take all this tension," he said.

The woman filled a tall glass from a bubbling orange juice dispenser. "Give me some money, Billy." Kevin turned to the waiting woman. "He's got it." Then to me. "Come on, come on, you'll get it back."

I threw a bill on the counter.

In the car again, I stared out the window. Cars rushed by, horns blaring. Kevin parked near the river. "Listen, Billy, Uncle Paul and Grandma Betty are taking you kids in. You ought to be grateful. They're doing it for us."

"For you, not for us. You're getting what you want. Dr. Keller!"

Kevin got out of the car. "Look, I don't want to be fighting with you. I know it's hard on you, but just remember it's hard on me, too."

He walked along the river with me following. Ahead there was an old brick tower. The river curved by the city like a leaden snake. I kicked a soda can ahead of me, then flattened it and kicked it again. He didn't care that the three of us were going off in

47

three different directions. Our family was coming apart like a cracked egg.

"You're an insensitive clod, you know that, Kevin? A Grade-A one-hundred-percent horse's ass."

"Meaning what?"

"Meaning. . . ." I waited for a couple pushing a carriage to pass. "Why don't you stay home?" I took a deep breath. Calm down, I told myself. Be as calm and reasonable as he is. "Just what I told you. Stay home, and we stay together. Go, and it's the end of the Kellers."

He walked away from me.

"Don't try to get away from me. If you stayed home, we could stay together. Yes," I shouted, going after him. "It's that simple."

"Baloney!" He shoved me off. "You're showboating. Stop dramatizing. What's so bad about you living with Uncle Paul? You and Lori won't be that far apart. Just because we're separated doesn't mean we're finished. You think just because Mom and Dad — " He looked out over the water. "I know you want to stay together," he said evenly. "I understand. I wish we could do it, but things don't always work out just because you want them to. Sometimes nothing works out. I don't have to tell you. Dad and Mom should have had fifty more years. You know what I was worried about, Billy? Dad's weight. I kept saying, Dad, stay off those prime steaks. They're full of fat, and don't drive so much. Get out there and walk. Tone up your heart."

"What's the point?"

"I don't know what the point is. I'm just talking.

You talked, now I'm talking. I called Mom the night before they went. I had a feeling something might happen, but I didn't say it because I'm a chronic worrier from way back. I worry when I get into an elevator or drive over a bridge, and I hate airplanes. But I didn't say, Don't go. I told Mom to take lots of pictures to show us when they came home."

"Okay. Okay."

Kevin removed his glasses and rubbed his eyes red. "I don't know . . . maybe you're right. Maybe I should stay home."

I waited, afraid to say anything.

"So I'll fall behind in school — that's not the end of the world. Only what are we going to do about money? Somebody'll have to work. Me. And what kind of money will I make? Not what Dad made."

"I'll work, too."

"And what do we do if somebody gets sick?"

"You're our doctor."

"I'm not a doctor yet! That's what we're talking about. Billy, I have four tough years ahead of me."

"We can do it," I said. "I'll drop out of school."

"Mom and Dad would really like that — two uneducated dummies. Look, Billy, I thought about it — everything you're talking about. I've got medical school to get through, then an internship and a residency. Lori's got six more years of school, you've got a couple. Then what about college for you and Lori? That's big bucks. I'm not Mom and Dad. I can't be. I'm me — I'm selfish! I want to finish college and go to medical school. Okay, I'm thinking about Kevin! What's so wrong with that? What are you thinking

49

about, but Billy Keller? Face it: You don't like change. You howled when Dad and Mom wanted to move here and now you're whining because you have to move again. Well, tough! I can't do anything about that." He threw off his jacket. "Leave me alone! I'm going to run."

I found a place out of the wind in the shelter of the brick tower and sat down, my hands in my jacket pockets. I remembered another cold winter day of blue skies and wind. Behind the elementary school in Delmar, Crazy Julius, a big kid nobody liked, started knocking me around. He said he was going to swing me around his head and see how far he could throw me.

I was so scared I peed in my pants. And then Kevin came charging in. I don't know where he came from. "That's my brother, you creep. Let go!"

No matter how I resented my brother sometimes, that's the way I imagined him. He was the rescuer, the one who always saved me. Even when he was mean he was saving me. The summer before last when I was fourteen and couldn't stand being around my family, I went to stay with Kevin where he was working on the shore at Ocean Heights. He wasn't that happy to see me. I had to sleep on the floor in his room, but he slipped me hamburgers when his boss wasn't around.

Kevin came jogging around the tower. "I'm thinking about it. I'm thinking about doing it."

Kevin, the rescuer. Did he mean it?

"I can go to school here. Go nights and work days."

50

"What about medical school?" Instead of agreeing with him, I started arguing with him. "What's Kathy going to say?"

"Let me worry about that. I can't figure you out, Billy. Where are the cheers?"

"All I hear so far is that you're thinking about it."

"You want me to write it out in blood?"

"Say it."

"Okay, it's settled."

"What's settled?"

"I'm staying."

I got to my feet. Scared, a little dizzy. I'd done it. I'd made him stay.

All the way back to the house, I kept thinking he'd change his mind when we got home, the way he used to when we were kids. Promise me a dollar to get me home and then "forget" he'd ever said it.

"You're going to do it," I said. "You said you were going to do it, and you're going to do it."

"You're pushing your luck, kid."

I slumped back in the seat, sure that he'd gone back on his word already. But I was wrong. The minute we walked into the house, he told them he wasn't going back to Boston. "I'll lose some school, but I can make it up."

"You mean you're going to stay?" Uncle Paul said. "After all the talking we did and working things out. You're not serious, Kevin. Think about it. You're not going to keep your schoolwork up. You can't take care of a family and go to school at the same time."

"Don't worry. I'm not leaving school. I know I'm going to lose a little. I'm going to have to work, but

51

I'll go to school. I'm not going to stop now."

If it had been me talking, or Lori, nobody would have paid any attention. But Kevin was older and he looked sensible. It was those gold-rimmed glasses. Even though Aunt Joan and Uncle Paul were doubtful at first, they took him seriously.

"Do you really think we should do this?" Aunt Joan kept saying. "How can we leave these children alone?"

"Poor Lori," Grandma Betty said. "She's just a child. I know she wants to come home with me."

Everybody turned to Lori. She hadn't said anything yet. "You don't want to stay alone with your brothers, do you?" Grandma Betty said. "You want to come home with me."

Lori hugged Grandma. "I want to stay here, Grandma," she said. "I love you, Grandma, but I want to stay with my brothers." She sat down on the couch next to me and poked me. "Billy," she whispered, "is it going to happen?"

I crossed my fingers.

Uncle Paul tugged at his collar. "It sure would simplify things if you stayed, Kevin. No house to sell, no packing up, no furniture to move. You're right, you can go to school here." He glanced at Aunt Joan. "We can help you out a little with money. The important thing is if you need us, we're not that far away. Just a phone call away." He looked around. "I was on my own when I was sixteen."

I thought everything was settled, when Grandma Betty suddenly said she'd stay with Lori and me, so Kevin could go back to school. For a few minutes everyone thought it was a great idea but Uncle Paul vetoed it. "It won't work. Lots of reasons. Money is a big one. We can't support this house and keep Kevin in school. We can help some but he's going to have to work. And your eyes, Ma — you know your health isn't that good."

We talked half the day. I thought they'd never agree, but Kevin convinced them. He threw himself into it, just kept talking and talking, giving all the reasons that it was the right decision. "I appreciate everything you've done for us, Uncle Paul. You, too, Aunt Joan, and Grandma, but this is what I think we should do. It's the right thing for our family." Once he'd made up his mind, it was like a game he had to win.

They stayed one more night. The next day, before they left, Aunt Joan went on a giant shopping spree. She packed the refrigerator and the cupboards with food and left big boxes of crackers and cereal under the kitchen table.

Chapter 8

Someone knocking at the door woke me. I was
sleeping on the living-room floor, Lori next to
me. We'd fallen asleep watching a late movie on TV.
Kevin was on the couch.

Knock-knock-knock. *Go away*. I pulled the blanket over my head. We'd been camping out in the living room with the shades pulled down and the TV on
ever since the relatives had left. Mom and Dad's
room was closed up. None of us went into it. It was
as if all our energy left with Uncle Paul and Aunt
Joan and we collapsed like weeds underwater, sunk
down in the gloom of the living room.

The relatives had left Monday. Today was Saturday . . . or Sunday . . . or some day. The principal's

secretary had called twice already and wanted to know how we were getting along. When were we coming back? Kevin talked to her. "They'll be coming to school soon," he said in that responsible, gold-rimmed voice.

"When do we have to go?" Lori said when he hung up.

"Whenever you're ready." He went back to his book. Did he care? Mom and Dad would have told us what to do.

I went to the door with the blanket wrapped around me. Mrs. Stein stood there, holding out a pot. "Mushroom barley soup?"

"What?" I pushed the hair out of my eyes.

"Mushroom barley soup. For you and your brother and sister." She handed me the pot of soup. "It's nearly noon. What are you children doing? Staying up all night? I hear the TV in the middle of the night. I can't understand how they leave children these days. Don't you have to go to school?"

"Tomorrow." Was tomorrow Monday? I felt ashamed standing there in a blanket, with my bare feet and my face unwashed. Mrs. Stein looked past me into the apartment. "Yes, well. . . ." I started closing the door, not wanting her to see the mess. "Thanks for the soup, Mrs. Stein."

I put the pot down on the floor in front of Kevin. He reached for his glasses. "What's that?"

"It smells good." Lori sniffed hungrily. She pushed up the sleeves of her red ski pajamas.

"Any crackers to go with it?" Kevin said.

"I'll go see." Lori ran to the kitchen and returned

with a sleeve of soda crackers and one spoon to share. "Last clean spoon."

Kevin crumbled crackers into the pot. "What are you doing to the soup?" I said. "I like liquid in my soup."

"Get me a cup, then."

I reached behind me and found a cup.

We took turns with the spoon and cleaned the pot out.

"What's today, Kevin?" Lori said.

"It's Saturday," I said. I'd finally figured it out because I heard the vacuum going downstairs. "Holly and Steve clean their apartment on Saturday."

"That's what we should do," Lori said. "Mom made us clean our rooms on Saturday, Kevin."

Kevin adjusted his glasses and reached for his book.

"Mom never let us lie around and watch TV on Saturday. You should make us clean up, Kevin, and go to school next week."

"Clean up," Kevin said. "Go to school." Then he went off to the bathroom with his book.

The house used to shine when Mom and Dad were here. Dad's ratty navy sweater hung on a nail in the broom closet with the black cowboy hat and rubber boots he wore when he washed the Mercedes. When Mom cleaned she wore an old pair of dad's jeans, tied up with a woven Indian belt. Even on Saturdays, she still managed to get a little darkroom time in, even if it was just hanging out a couple of sheets of contacts to dry. At the end of the day the house was cleaner, something was fixed, the Mercedes shone. Good smells, pie and paint and furniture polish.

Lori and I put the living room back together, maybe not the way Mom did it, but it looked better than before. "Why don't you get dressed," I said. "Let's wash up."

"What about you? Your feet stink."

"Thanks for telling me. I'm going to take a shower."

Later Lori got out her guitar and I sat by the window looking out. Holly carried out their garbage and put it in the can in front, then yelled to Steve to let her in. I opened the window. "Hi, Holly, lock yourself out?"

She rubbed her bare arms. "I'm always doing that, locking myself out. Hi, Billy, how are you feeling? Doing okay?"

"Yes," I said, leaning out. "I'm going back to school Monday."

"Just take your time, whatever you do." She waved and went back inside.

Kevin was on the phone in the hall. When he saw me, he pulled the phone into the closet. "Talking to Kathy?" I said, walking by. It was no secret. She was in school in Boston and they were on the phone almost every day. He didn't make a decision without talking to her first. What college he should transfer to down here, and how he was going to get the rest of his clothes and books from school, and what he should eat for supper tonight and breakfast tomorrow morning, and for all I knew if he should brush his teeth or not. What worried me was that Kathy wasn't thrilled about his staying with us. Kevin told us that himself.

"Who's she to say?" Lori said. "She's not our family."

"She will be someday," Kevin said.

"Hoo-hoo. When's that going to be?"

"When we're both through with medical school — if I ever get there."

"Sorry you're not there with her, instead of being stuck here with us?" I asked.

"No comment.

"Let's go to the movies," Kevin said. That was a surprise. He and Kathy had probably talked about how to keep the natives happy. What was an even bigger surprise was when he handed me the Mercedes key. He hadn't let me touch the car since he'd come home.

"I want to see *Halloween*," Lori said. "Maryanne says it's really scary."

"Who's Maryanne?"

"She's my friend in school. She saw it six times."

"If your friend saw that movie six times her brains must be scrambled."

But *Halloween* was what we saw. In the theater we bought chocolate and Ju-Ju's. All through the movie some maniac with a double-edged axe chased a terrified woman, breaking up furniture and splitting doors apart. In the middle of the movie I walked out.

I sat in the car. I could still hear the woman in the movie screaming.

Going home after the movie, we all jammed together in the front seat, not talking, all of us moody. Kevin had his arm around Lori. I concentrated on the driving, timing the lights ahead so I got to them just as they turned green, not thinking about anything but the lights.

When we got to our house, the windows facing the streets were all lit up. I heard voices. I did hear voices! "They're back!" I left the car in the middle of the street and ran into the house, Lori after me.

"Mom and Dad!" For a moment I thought my heart was going to explode.

Then it was over. There was nobody in the house. We'd left the lights and the TV on. Kevin turned on me. "Look what you did to Lori. She's shaking."

"I'm sorry." I couldn't look at them. I went down the hall toward my room, but even then I couldn't help looking in every room, in the dark places, hoping and praying for the miracle.

Chapter 9

On the first day of school, Lori and I stood across the street a long time before we crossed over. The school looked like a prison to me, gray and gritty, with grates on all the windows. The junior and senior highs were joined by a long enclosed walkway everyone called the Yellow Brick Road. Behind it the dome of the pool rose like a bald green head.

"You think it's going to be bad?" Lori said. "Everybody's going to know, aren't they?"

"Maybe." Relax, I told myself. Somebody asks you a question, answer them. There's been a death in the family. Keep it cool. A death in the family. That's all you have to say.

Today was the day we were all starting fresh. Kevin

had been really flying this morning, talking a blue streak. "You kids are going to school, right? You got your keys? Money? Keep an eye on each other." Then he'd gone off looking for work, and to register for a couple of classes.

Lori saw her friend Sam, the girl she'd played basketball with, and called to her to wait up. "That's Maryanne with Sam."

"The tall one? She's your age?"

"I told you she was built. You won't forget to meet me, will you?"

"On the Yellow Brick Road."

The school smelled stale, like old egg-salad sandwiches. "How you doing?" Eugene Connors said. He was a short black kid who had the locker next to mine. "I haven't seen you for a while."

"Ri-ight." I started throwing things out of my locker, looking for my schedule. I'd forgotten what classes I was supposed to go to.

"Spring cleaning?" Eugene said. "That's what I ought to do."

"Ri-ight." I pitched everything back in and the blue schedule card fell out. Homeroom, then history, then English.

"Billy Keller," Mrs. Rath said when I walked into homeroom. "I heard the terrible news." Her eyes shimmered with sympathy and mascara. "Are you all right, Billy?" She held my hand. I felt everyone's eyes on the back of my neck.

At my desk I sat and yawned. My eyes teared. I wiped them quickly, afraid someone would think I was crying.

61

LJ Braun sat down next to me. "How's it going, man?" I was afraid he was going to say something about my parents. He had called the house while I was out of school. I appreciated his calling me then — I was glad he called. "I hear you got big trouble," he'd said. But I didn't want to talk about it now, not here, not in school.

"I'm okay," I said. "How about you? How was your weekend?"

"We had a beer blast." LJ's large pimply face broke into a grin. He seemed relieved, too. "My family went to Washington for the weekend. My mother and —" He paused, frowned, looked grim and worried. "Am I talking too much? Tell me to shut up if I am."

He was being nice to me — too nice. That wasn't LJ's style. Why didn't he punch me in the arm the way he normally did? Was that wrong? Was I acting wrong? Was I too matter-of-fact? I remembered a girl in Delmar whose father had died suddenly and how she'd cried in class. The teacher had to take her out of the room. I didn't want to cry in front of other people. Did that mean I was lacking feeling?

In Mr. Donald's history class, the lights were dimmed, the shades drawn, a white screen raised in front. I slipped to the back where LJ was sitting and put my head down on the desk. "Wake me when the war's over."

The movie started. A booming voice filled the room, talking about World War II, about the German raids over London. I shut my eyes, thought I wouldn't look, but then I looked. Saw the bombs fall,

62

saw the land turn to clouds of smoke and dust. Heard sirens . . . saw people running.

The explosions vibrated through my jaw and teeth, rocked through my skull. I hung on to the desk, waiting for it to end.

In English, Miss Castallani, the sexiest teacher in school, sat down next to me. That wasn't bad, Miss Castallani that close, covering me with her perfume. LJ, behind me, was breathing like a dog.

"Billy," she said, putting her face close to mine, like we were sharing secrets.

Say something, make an understanding noise. She's putting herself out for you. It hurts her to think about you. Thank her, tell her you're getting along fine. But I couldn't speak.

"Billy, is there anything I can do to help you?" She sat there with me, almost cheek to cheek. I got excited. I couldn't help it, and then I felt like an animal.

Right after lunch I was called to the office. I ran because my first thought was Lori. On the way down the stairs, I bumped into a guy coming the other way. "Sorry," I said and started past him.

He grabbed me by my shirt. "What are you, blind?"

I twisted free and ran. In the office I saw that the front of my shirt was torn, two buttons gone. I was suddenly so hot I wanted to go back and kill that guy.

In the office, they told me Mr. Anderson, the principal, wanted to see me. "Go right in."

Mr. Anderson stood up and shook hands with me. He was a huge man. I'd never talked to him before.

"Sit down, Billy." On his desk there was a picture of a round-faced woman and two round-faced kids. "I'm glad you're back in school. Routine can be the best therapy. Of course, the magnitude of your loss . . . both your parents . . . terrible, terrible."

I tried to keep that neutral look that had gotten me through the day so far. I focused on the schedule board behind him.

"If there is anything I or any of my staff can do — anytime things get to be too much for you and you need to talk, day or night, don't hesitate. My door is always open. Call me at home." He jotted down a number on a yellow slip of paper and I put it in my shirt pocket.

"Don't lose it now. I don't give everyone my number."

I started to get up.

"Sit down, Billy, don't rush away. Who's home with you now?"

"My older brother."

"He's taken over in your parents' place?" Mr. Anderson joined his hands together. He wore a heavy gold ring on each hand. "How old is your brother? Is he married?" When I said Kevin was a student, Mr. Anderson jotted something down on a pad. "Any other relatives you can turn to? Does your brother plan to work? What about school? Is he going to school here?"

His questions made me nervous. He wanted to know everything that was going on at home. Was he going to say we couldn't stay together because Kevin didn't qualify as a parent? Could a principal do that?

When it was time to go he stood up and put his arm across my shoulders and gave me a parting squeeze.

"This is the test, isn't it? Life's test for each of us. We all have to face it sooner or later. Unfortunately, in your case it came too soon."

For the rest of the day I walked through the corridors with blinders on. I didn't want another teacher to pull me aside or see another caring look. Part of me didn't want anybody to know, but another part of me wanted everybody to say, *Hey, look at that kid, look at the way he's holding himself. See how straight his back is, how jaunty, how light he is on his feet? You've got to admire his courage, ladies and gentlemen. Don't you think he deserves a round of applause?*

After school, I met Lori on the Yellow Brick Road and we went home without speaking much. She looked the way I felt, as if somebody had stepped on her.

Chapter 10

Not a day passed that I didn't go home without that thin edge of hope pushing through me. The longer I was away from the house, the stronger the feeling grew. Maybe . . . maybe this time. . . . It was always the same, no matter how many times I caught myself at it. It had nothing to do with reason. As I went up the steps, I held my breath, my heart high in my throat, and then I'd walk in the house, into those dark rooms.

Everything was a mess. Clothes everywhere — on the floor, chairs, hanging on doorknobs and the tops of doors. Kevin had posted a work schedule for the week on the refrigerator but none of us stuck to it. All we did was bicker about who was supposed to do what. The little we did always seemed to come undone the minute after we finished. Even when we put things away in the bureaus and closets and cupboards, as soon as we turned our backs, everything popped out again and things were just as bad as they were before.

Kevin complained constantly. "Mom worked and took care of the house and did the meals, the whole bit."

"Don't talk about Mom," Lori said.

"Sorry, but you get the idea."

"What about you?" I said. "I don't see you doing that much."

"You don't think looking for work is work? You go out and try it. And another thing. Look at all the lights on in this house. It's not even dark yet. And the garbage." There were boxes of it in the hall. He pulled out a half-eaten pizza and a loaf of bread that had gone moldy. "That's money I'm not earning yet."

"You said that already."

"I'll say it again. I'm not earning yet."

Aunt Joan and Uncle Paul were calling every few days. We took turns talking to them. "How are you, Billy?" Aunt Joan said when it was my turn. "You sound stuffed up."

"I've got a little cold, that's all, Aunt Joan."

"How about Lori? How is she?" There was always that little extra worry in her voice when she asked about Lori.

"She's okay," I said. "How about you, Aunt Joan? How's Grandma Betty?"

Then Kevin got on the line and the first thing he

said was that he still wasn't working and we were probably going to have to borrow. "Just till I'm working, Aunt Joan. I wouldn't ask otherwise."

"Are we really short?" I asked Kevin when he hung up.

"No, I asked her because we're rolling in bucks."

He blew up over everything. "Who threw my denim jacket on the floor?" he yelled. To hear him, you'd think someone had done it on purpose. I didn't know if I'd knocked it over.

"The hooks in this house are slippery," I said.

"Pick it up," Kevin said.

He really made an issue of it. I was tempted to tell him to shove it, but every time he got mad, I got a little worried. Was this going to be his excuse for packing up his knapsack and moving out?

I picked the jacket up. "Satisfied, Hitler?"

So we squabbled, but mostly we were getting along. The only sour note was that days and then a couple weeks passed and Kevin still didn't have a job. He could have had kitchen jobs in Arby's or Burger King — he was an experienced short order cook — but he was fussy. He wanted the right job, the right hours, afternoons or nights only, because he'd enrolled for a couple of courses in the morning at the Extension College.

Things were getting better in school. Lori had her friends — Sam and Maryanne — and people had stopped treating me like a freak. Well, actually, they still stiffened and glazed over when they saw me. Only LJ was normal and even he would get a pained, worried look on his big face if he accidentally said something about his parents in front of me. LJ was skipping lunches to take weight off and we were going swimming together fifth period.

I loved diving; I loved going up, that lifting, light, flying sensation. I stepped out on the diving board, tried the spring a couple of times. The plastic bubble over the pool cast a green underwater light over everything. I wanted to do something both good and ordinary, a normal dive.

Swimmers churned the water below, the coach yelled, and from somewhere I heard LJ's high cackle. One, two, three, up and away. . . . Was this what it was like for them, that last moment? I forgot to reach for my toes and hit the water hard.

"Hey, Keller, over here." LJ's big, familiar hand pulled me up. "How are you doing, man? Guys, this is my country cousin, Billy Keller. What kind of dive was that, cous?"

I stood, dripping water on the tiles. LJ made room for me in the circle. "Hey, Ralph." LJ pulled one of his friends around. "You see those cheeks Keller's got? That's from living in cow country. Am I right, cousin? These brothers don't know what country living is. Ralph, do you know what a cow pie is?"

"Sure, that's what cows eat for dessert."

LJ nudged me. "Me and my cousin here are going to bring back a trailerload of juicy cow pies and sell them for an after-school snack."

I rubbed at a fleck of blue paint on my trunks. Last summer, before we'd moved from Delmar (was it only last summer?), I'd painted our garage door. It was a hot day and I worked in my bathing suit. Mom had wanted to paint the garage white like the rest of the house, but Dad said blue to cover all the ball marks. I finally painted it like a checkerboard, blue and white, each square a different color. "It looks cheesy," Mom said, which meant it lacked class. But Dad laughed and said we'd leave it that way.

Later, when we were dressed, I stood with LJ at the end of the corridor that led to the pool. LJ kept nudging me, clutching my arm, then pinching me on the butt. "See her? . . . Uh, nice. . . . That one, too."

Then a girl wearing a blue military-style tunic came toward us. Red lips, eyes dark with makeup, short blond hair tucked behind her ears — she stood out in the grayness like a tropical bird.

"Hi!" I said. The way she moved, the click of her heels, everything about her was full of authority. "Hi, there!"

She ignored me. "Who's that?" I asked LJ.

"Margaret Geri. Nice, huh? Forget it, she's a senior. You're too green and ignorant for her."

The bell rang. I walked along with Margaret, a step behind her. Margaret. Margaret Geri. *How are you, Margaret? How are you, Billy? Nice to meet you. That's not the half of it, Margaret. You don't know it yet, but we're going to be friends.*

The bell rang again. She looked back, as though she'd known I was there all along, and winked at me.

The halls filled; I was carried along on the flood. She had winked at me. That wink! It made me happier than it should have. Happier than I deserved to be. Should I be watching girls, following them? Was it soon enough? Too soon? Had enough time passed?

Oh, the possibilities of that wink. It was no squint, no speck of dirt in her eye. The wink had been for me. A wink to let me know that she was aware of me, of my attention. My liking her was all right, that wink said. She liked it. She liked me.

Seeing Margaret changed my luck. The very next day Kevin came home with good news. "Gather round, my little chickens. You're looking at a working man. A wage earner. Ten guys wanted that job and I got it."

"How much are you making?" I asked. "Is it a night job?"

"Guess." He had a bag of goodies with him and he started pulling out sandwiches and packaged cakes.

"You're going to be manager of Burger King," Lori said.

"No, no, Lori," I said, "you're looking at a president. What'd they do, give you a bank? No, let me guess again. They gave you a food market. Or is it a little more humble than that? You're wiping tables at Burger King."

"I'm a paramedic on an ambulance," Kevin said. And when we didn't appreciate the importance of it, he told us it was medical work, as close to doctors as he could hope to get right now. "Terrific experience. All those broken bodies to fix."

"That's disgusting," Lori said.

"Hey, just joking, honey," Kevin said. "How do you think doctors get their experience?"

"Very funny!" She started to leave the room, but Kevin went after her and brought her back. He wasn't going to let anything spoil his party.

"I know I've been obnoxious lately," he said, "but that's all over with now that I have a job." He sat Lori down in front of the bag of goodies. "You choose first. Which sandwich do you want? Or do you want Cheese Bits? No? Fritos? Soda?" He kept pulling things out of the bag like Santa Claus. "How about this half gallon of ice cream? All you get is a lick, Billy and I are going to demolish it."

Lori laughed. It was a real party after that.

Chapter 11

The bearded man at the door wore a bulky white sweater and a black cap. "Kevin Keller?" He looked uncertainly at the card in his hand.

He looked vaguely familiar — bulging eyes and rough red skin — like someone I'd seen in the neighborhood collecting for a charity. He stuck out his hand. I handed him a dollar. He laughed. "I know we social workers don't make much. Are you Billy? My name's Milo Miller. I'm from Children's Services. Your school asked me to check in with you."

I panicked. "My brother's not home." But it was too late. He was inside, looking around the living room. And what a mess it was. Kevin's bedding on the couch, cups and boxes of cereal on the TV. A curtain was half off the rod.

He craned his neck, looking at everything. "Nice place you've got here. I've always liked these brownstones. High ceilings and tall windows. Nice, nice, but they cost big bucks. How are you making out with money? Any problems?"

"No problems."

He took off his cap, then glanced at the card. "You rent two apartments. How's that working out?"

"No problems." Did he believe me? Everything I said sounded like a lie.

"The only income you show is social security payments and the two rentals."

"My brother's working. And we're fixing up another apartment upstairs. I'm working on it." I hadn't been up there since the funeral service.

"Oh, good." He dug around in his pockets. "You don't happen to have a pencil I could borrow?"

"Wait, I'll get one." But he was right behind me with that apologetic smile and those big busy eyes. "Nice. Nice kitchen."

Nice! What was wrong with this guy? Was he blind? Couldn't he smell? There was a week's garbage in the corner and you couldn't see the table for the dirty dishes. I found him a pencil stub. "You caught us at the wrong time. I was just going to clean up."

He moved a pair of jeans off a chair and sat down. "You have a younger sister." He turned his card over. "Lori? How is that spelled? Is she at home?" It sounded like an accusation, like why *isn't* she at home?

"She's at a friend's house. Sam — that's a girl," I said quickly.

"You kids must get along real well. No fighting?"

"Fight? No — never." Nobody was going to believe that. "We argue a little — not much."

"I know how that is," Miller said. "I used to fight with my kid brother all the time." And then he wrote something down.

Everything was on that card. All his questions. All my answers. Were we in touch with our relatives? How often did we see them? Were they helping us out? One question after another. "What about school, Billy? How're you doing?"

"Fine."

"It hasn't been easy for you."

"I'm all right," I said. "I keep my marks up."

Milo Miller scratched his beard. "I'm sure it hasn't been easy for any of you. I don't know if you kids are gutsy or nuts. It seems to me of the options you had open, you chose the toughest one. Losing your parents is probably the most profoundly stressful situation a kid can be in. And then to take the burden of this house and supporting yourselves on top of that. . . ." He shook his head. "I don't know if you kids are going to be able to get away with it."

Then Lori came in. Her braid was coming apart and her coat was buttoned up wrong. She looked like one of those neglected kids. "Hi, Lori," Miller said, like he was family. "How's it going? I'm Milo Miller. You look like you've had a hard day."

"What?" Her face twitched and she started chewing her lip. Then without a word she walked out of the room.

"She's shy," I said.

75

Miller nodded. "Early adolescence," he said and jotted something down. He couldn't make a move without that card. "Well. . . ." He put the card away and stood up. "I'd better get going." He put on his cap. "It's been a nice visit. Next time we'll talk some more."

"Why?" I said.

"Why what?"

"Why are you coming back?"

He laughed. "You don't beat around the bush, do you, Billy. I haven't met Kevin yet." He held out his hand. "Nice meeting you, Billy."

I followed him to the front door and watched him walk down the street.

Lori came out of her room. "Is he gone? I didn't like him. You want something to eat?"

"No! You were supposed to wash the dishes." Her face closed up but I couldn't think about her. Miller was on my mind. He'd been here five minutes and thought he had us all figured out. *Of the options you had, you took the worst one!* What did he know about it? We were doing fine. Did he think breaking us up wouldn't hurt us? Maybe everyone else was waiting for him to tell them what to do but we weren't.

I was still up, still agitated when Kevin came home. He was in his ambulance whites. The first thing he did was make himself a sandwich. "You want some?" I shook my head and told him about Miller. He took a bite of his sandwich. "Who'd you say this guy was?"

Didn't he hear anything I said? "The school sent him. He's from Children's Services. What are we going to do, Kevin? You know the government. If they want to take your property, all they have to do is condemn it and you're out."

"Great example," Kevin said, crumpling the bag.

"You're not worried?"

"Why should I be? What'd he say? He just came for a visit."

"What if he comes back?"

"He probably won't. He saw what he wanted to see. I'm bushed. How about getting out of here so I can go to sleep."

The next morning — it was Saturday — I was home alone when there was a knock at the door. Miller! "One minute!" I raced through the house, throwing things into closets and behind doors. In the kitchen I cleared the table, shoved the dirty dishes into the cupboard. Kevin's books I jammed into the fridge.

I went to the door, smoothed my hair, tucked in my shirt. *Sorry, Mr. Miller, I was just getting dressed.*

"Hi, Billy," Holly said.

I slumped against the door. "Am I glad to see you!"

"I'm glad someone is. Steven and I are having a fight. Can I take refuge with you?" She followed me into the living room.

"What are you fighting about?"

"You wouldn't believe it, it's so dumb. I told him he ate with his mouth open and he got mad. . . . Oh, I don't want to talk about it. Offer me a cup of tea."

In the kitchen I started the water heating, found

some tea bags and a few crackers. "Not much left. We're eating the paint off the walls. Want some orange marmalade? It's in the refrigerator."

"What's this?" Holly said, opening the refrigerator door. "Books!"

"Kevin's hot books," I said. "He keeps them cool in there."

"Kevin is peculiar."

"Yeah, he is." But then I told the truth. "I put them there." Then I had to tell her how I thought she was Miller from Children's Services and how I'd pushed everything out of sight to make a good impression. "We're keeping the place neat now."

"I noticed," she said, picking up an empty Rice Krispies box off the chair. Then we sat around and talked till Steve came looking for her.

Chapter 12

In the middle of his second week on the job Kevin told us he needed a break. Friday he was taking off work and going to Boston for the weekend to see Kathy.

He left Thursday night. It was the first time since he'd come home that we'd been separated. Six weeks had gone by. Friday morning I woke up with the most desolate feeling. I'd dreamed Kevin was dead. When I looked in the living room and saw the empty couch, it hit me all over again. *He's gone, and he isn't coming back.*

It had nothing to do with sense. He said he was coming back. But all I could think was that now we had two empty rooms, Mom and Dad's room, and the living room where Kevin slept. After school that day I hung around outside, hoping to see Margaret. It was a warm day, the sun was melting the snow. I spent a long time in the playground watching a basketball game.

Finally I went home. As I came up the steps to the house the living-room window opened and someone squirted me with water. Lori was home with Sam and Maryanne. Maryanne looked older than both Sam and Lori; I didn't quite know why. It was something about the way she looked at me, like she dared me to say anything.

"What are you preteens up to?"

"Preteens?" Maryanne hooted. "Check that out!" The three of them were in the living room, armed with water pistols.

"Listen to the senior citizen," Lori said.

"We're having a party," Sam said in her husky voice. She sprawled on a chair holding a water pistol over her eyes. "Want to come?"

"Shut up, Sam," Maryanne said. Secret looks shot back and forth.

"What party? What's going on?" I said. "No party here without my permission." I ignored Lori's outraged expression. "I'm in charge here."

"Since when?" Lori said.

"Since Kevin's away." Maryanne lit a cigarette. "And no smoking in this house." I took the cigarette from her mouth and flipped it out the window.

Maryanne fiddled with her water pistol. "You're just like my brother. You need to be cooled off." She squirted me in the face and yelled, "Get him."

I grabbed Sam's pistol and squirted Maryanne. They came at me and I ducked down behind the couch. It was kid stuff. Captain Billy against the Savages. Sam batted me with a pillow. I laughed and squirted her. Maryanne dumped a plastic pail of water over my head. She was crazy. She doused the whole living room.

I made a grab for her. She was the one I wanted to get but I slipped and went down. They piled on me, three on one. Maryanne grabbed my hair and yanked my head back. Sam held one arm and Lori the other. They had me flat out, spread-eagled, when Miller walked in.

"Hello, anybody home?" He was at the open door. "It looks like you're having a regular party." He picked up a soggy pillow and put it on the windowsill.

I got to my feet, tucked my shirt in. There was water all over the floor.

"Nice group you've got here." His eyes were like a TV camera. I could hear the report. *On my regular visitation to the Keller house, Billy Keller, age sixteen, was on the floor, and his sister, Lori Keller, age twelve, and two of her girl friends were beating him. This appears to be an unsupervised house.*

"Is Kevin in today?" Miller said. "I'd like to talk to him."

"He's working." I glanced at Lori.

"This early? I thought he worked nights."

"They called him in. There was an emergency." One lie followed another.

"You have a little clean-up to do before your brother comes home." He put on his cap. "Just tell Kevin I was here. I'll be back."

That night I called Kevin in Boston. Kathy answered the phone. "Kevin's taking a nap, Billy. Is something wrong?"

"No, I just want to talk to Kevin." Just checking in, I thought, but when I heard his voice I blurted out that Miller had been here and he was coming back.

"So what?" Kevin said.

"He wants to talk to you. I didn't tell him you were in Boston."

"It's no secret. I can go to Boston without his permission."

After I hung up, I found one of the water pistols under a chair and smashed it under my foot. What was Kevin doing in Boston, anyway? I remembered Kathy in those white overalls and white sneakers, charming Mom and Dad. Laughing gull Kathy, good Doctor Kathy. If it wasn't for her, Kevin would be here right now.

Kevin came home Sunday night, walked in, wearing his gray jogging outfit.

"What'd you do, run all the way from the station?" I said. "I would have come down and picked you up. The Mercedes is just rotting out there on the street."

Kevin pulled off his sweat shirt. There was a silver pendant on the chain around his neck.

"Did Kathy give that to you?" I reached for it.

"Hands off." His first words.

"You're in a great mood, Kevin," I said.

Seeing Kathy hadn't improved his disposition at all. He was in a bad mood for a couple of days. Tuesday night he came home early and really blew up. Lori and I were watching TV on the couch. His blanket was on the floor, just the edge of it.

"Billy! Pick this up! I told you kids to leave my blankets alone!"

Lori picked up the blanket and started to spread it on the couch. Kevin grabbed it out of her hand. "I want you kids out of here. I'm going to sleep." Then he started yelling again about not getting enough sleep on this crummy couch, and how nobody cared, and the house was a pigpen, and how was he going to keep working and taking classes if he didn't get enough sleep.

"You want my room?" I said. "You can have it. Take it."

"No, I don't want your room. I want my own room." He wrapped himself in the blanket. "You know where I want to sleep."

"You can't have Mom and Dad's room," Lori said instantly.

"I need it, Lori. I need my sleep. How long am I supposed to go on sleeping on the living-room couch?" he yelled. "There's no privacy in the living room. I can hear every move you kids make."

"We're quiet," Lori said. "I'm quiet."

"Yeah, so is a herd of elephants."

I hated it when Kevin started screaming and throwing his weight around. He was like a car without a driver. Where was the cool head? "I told you,

you can have my bed," I said. "I'll sleep on the floor."

"Forget it," Kevin said. "There's an empty room in the house and I want it. What if Kathy comes for a visit?"

"Not Mom and Dad's room." Lori got in front of Kevin, her arms spread. "You can't have it. She can sleep in my room."

"Great. Look, Lori, I know how you feel about Mom and Dad's room — I felt that way, too, but you've got to get over it."

"Take my room. Take it!"

"Are we going to live like people or what? I want a place of my own to sleep in, a room with a door on it that I can close and have some privacy without having everyone walking all over me." He tried to put his arm around Lori. "You know, I'm working now, I'm working hard, I need a place to study."

Lori shook him off. "Take it, then," she said. "But you can't move anything."

"Lori, their furniture's got to go."

"Okay, Kevin, okay," I said. I could hear Kathy's voice in everything Kevin said. "It's your room, you do anything you want with it." I glanced at Lori. She was biting her braid, her face turned away from both of us. "Is it okay, Lori?"

"Leave me out of it," she said and walked out.

Chapter 13

Every day it seemed like I had to fight with Kevin over the Mercedes. It was his Boston mood — the why-didn't-I-stay-where-I-was-appreciated mood. I wasn't just harassing him. The car had to be moved every twenty-four hours. He collected a couple of tickets before he caught on and even then he was always parking it at the last minute and in places that made me want to scream. "Billy, I've got to take the spots I can find. I can't spend all afternoon. Anyway, you're a fanatic about that car."

"And you're trying to kill it, Kevin. Parking it on the corner where any idiot coming around too sharp could run right into it." The places he picked! In front of the school where kids were always throwing things. Or by the stores where they piled the garbage every night.

With the good weather, I started washing the car every day. Maybe I just liked running water. Not true. I loved the Mercedes and it bothered me that Kevin didn't and nobody was using it. Every morning it was covered with a new layer of grit.

I got out the hose and pail, washed and then rinsed the Mercedes. Water dripped from the fenders and I remembered Mom and Dad driving around on Sundays, Lori and me in the backseat with the red armrest down between us. There'd always be something good at the end of the day, a hot dog or ice cream. I wiped down the car, saw my face in the hood's dark mirror and behind it the house and the sky. I couldn't look up without thinking of them.

I'd just finished wringing out the rags when Kevin got into the car. He'd stayed home a couple of days from work with a cold. "I'm going over to West Market. Stick around for Lori."

"What are you going there for?" West Market was where all the car lots were.

"I want to find out what the Mercedes is worth." He must have seen on my face what I thought of that. "You got it looking so good — "

Alarms went off in my head. "You're not selling our car." I jumped into the car. I wasn't letting him out of my sight.

He drove to a car lot on West Market that specialized in used foreign cars. A trailer office in back displayed a big sign — TOYS FOR BOYS. I sat in the car while Kevin talked to the salesman.

Why was he thinking about selling the car? I knew he didn't love the Mercedes the way I did. Were we short of money? He'd missed some time from work, and then he was out with a cold for a couple of days. Why didn't he say something to me? I'd work.

The salesman came out and looked the car over. "What happened here?" he said, looking closely at a fender.

I stuck my head out the window. "The car's been in a wreck," I said. "Tell him, Kevin, the frame's bent."

The salesman smiled. "Your friend's got a sense of humor." He got in and started the engine. He wore a silver ID bracelet with his name on it. Don Porter. Maybe he got lost a lot and forgot his name. He hardly listened to the engine, turned the radio on and off. What did that prove? "Kevin," he said, "would you like to trade up this afternoon?"

Trade up. He had nothing on this lot that was in the class of our Mercedes.

"Do you owe anything on this one, Kevin?"

"No, I don't, Don."

Don and Kevin. I groaned.

Don and Kevin walked around the lot. I trailed along to protect my brother from Don the shark. "You think if I can get you a good deal we can trade today, Kevin? You've got enough in your car for a down payment." He stood with a hand on the hood of a neat little red MG. Its black leather interior was all cracked. Then he showed us an orange BMW with rust around the bottom of the doors. "These cars both have lots of zip."

"Listen," I said, pushing in, "all we want to know

is what you'll give us for our car. We don't even want to sell it to you, but if we did, how much?"

Don looked troubled. Oh, he really looked sad. "I'd like to help you boys out, but I don't think I could get you much on that car. It's not a good time for old cars, and it's sort of beat up."

"Beat up! That car is in perfect shape. What are you talking about? It'll run circles around any piece of junk you've got on this lot."

"What did you have to start yelling for?" Kevin said when we got back to the car. He took a tissue from his pocket and blew his nose. "I just wanted to hear what he was offering."

"You found out, didn't you? These dealers won't give you anything unless you buy up."

"Look, Billy, you're buggy about this car. Pay attention. A car in the city is expensive and the insurance is sky high, and it's a pain to drive."

"Look, I'll go to work if we need money. Just don't sell the Mercedes. It's our car, too, Kevin. Mine and Lori's." My voice shook. I was such an idiot about that car. "It's our family's car, not just yours. You can think what you want, but you can't sell it without our permission."

Kevin just sat there, breathing through his mouth, not saying anything.

"It's our father's car," I said. "Follow? Our father . . . our father." And then unable to stop myself, I said, "Our father who art in heaven. . . . Yes, our father, our father. He sees you, Kevin, whatever you do, he knows it. So don't pull any dirty deals."

Chapter 14

By accident I discovered that Margaret Geri worked at the CYO. I went over there Saturday morning looking for a game and saw Margaret in the basket room giving out towels. I thought she recognized me, but she didn't let on and I didn't have the nerve to start a conversation.

No game, but I shot baskets alone for a while, thinking about what I was going to say to Margaret when I went upstairs. *How's it going? How are you doing?* Really clever stuff. I wanted to impress Margaret, not sound like a jerk, and I finally left without saying anything.

At home I went straight to the unfinished upstairs

apartment. I was worried about Miller. The next time he turned up, it would be good to take him up here and show him that we weren't just living here — we were making things better. Even if it wasn't finished, there'd be progress. Every day I'd come up here and do something. The wiring first, then the Sheetrock, and then the finishing touches on the walls. After that, I'd hang the kitchen cabinets.

Going up the stairs I had the whole job worked out. It only took seconds to finish it in my mind. Then I opened the apartment door. I got a blast of cold air. Wires hung down from the ceiling where Dad had torn out the partitions. The windows were gray with dust. Boxes of broken plaster were piled near the door. Dad had asked me to carry them down to the street months ago.

I took the broom and started poking around at the debris. A gray, dusty, wood, and plaster smell rose around me. *Get the lead light, Billy, so you can see what you're doing.* Dad had said it to me a thousand times.

Something small and breathy brushed by me. Scared me. It was Shulty, the Steins' dog, sniffing around. "Shulty, you dirty dog."

Then Mr. Stein came wheezing up the stairs. "Who's up here? I'm coming up. Uhr! Uhr! Oh, it's you, Billy. Shulty heard a noise." He looked around. "A lot of work still to be done."

"I'm going to do it," I said. I put on my father's denim apron. When I'd worked with Dad I'd been tool fetcher, sweeper, and garbage lugger. Now I had the whole job to do myself.

"Now you look like a real worker." Mr. Stein nodded approvingly, then lit a bent cigarette. "You don't smoke, do you? Good." He pointed downstairs. "We don't say anything about this cigarette. Mrs. Stein thinks I'm killing myself smoking. She's right, but mum's the word. If she finds out, she'll never let me out of her sight."

Mr. Stein held the lead light while I tried to trace the wires for the kitchen. "As long as I don't have to move off my duff, I can help," he said. "I can't do the work but I can give you lots of advice."

The time went fast. Mr. Stein talked. "It's good to have work like this. You sit around, you think too much."

Around noon Kevin came home from the library. "Billy, you want to add anything to this shopping list? I'm going to the market now."

"Wait, I'll call Lori. She wants to go with us."

"I don't need your help."

"Yes, you do." I was feeling good. I'd actually gotten something done upstairs. "We don't trust you, my leader. Should we take the Mercedes?"

"Five blocks?"

"My leader, the car is just collecting dust on the street. If we drive we'll get done faster. I have many things to do today."

"A little exercise will do you good."

"Come on, Kevin, don't be so cheap."

We jogged to the market.

Lori was waiting for us in front of the Big M Market with her pal Maryanne, who was smoking. They were wearing identical yellow-knit hats with a red stripe and were twirling yellow yo-yos. Maryanne

91

doused her cigarette as soon as she saw us. I didn't think Kevin noticed.

Lori had been spending more and more time with Maryanne. First thing in the morning it was Maryanne on the phone waking Lori up, then Maryanne in school, then Maryanne after school. Why didn't Lori pal around more with Sam? I liked her a lot better. There was something straightforward about her. She was a kid and she acted like a kid. Every time I saw her around school, she gave me a big hello.

Inside the market, Kevin checked items off his list.

"Let's get Pop Tarts for breakfast," Lori said.

"No junk food. If it isn't on the list we don't buy it."

"Kevin, you are a dog," I said,

"You want the job?"

"Somebody has to be the dog in charge and you're it, Kevin." It was down to basics with Dr. K. Tuna fish and leafy greens.

"Pick up that Velveeta for toasted cheese?" Kevin told Lori.

"How about some Swiss cheese?" I said. "And mustard. We're out."

"We've got enough Swiss," Kevin said.

When the big cheese wasn't looking, I threw in a package of English muffins. Lori countered with a jar of dill pickles. I came back with a bag of potato chips and Lori jammed home a package of Fritos. He must have seen it but he didn't say anything. With all his sermons he ate the same junk we did.

"Peanuts, Lori." I threw her a bag. She threw it back to me. I backed up and ran into someone.

"Ooops." I turned around. It was Miller, pushing a shopping cart — Mr. Miller, in a bulging green sweater. "Billy," he said. "And Lori. How are you guys? This is nice."

This was the last place I had expected to see him. Had he been watching us all this time? Had he been making notes on us on his little card? *They bicker a lot . . . loud . . . display inappropriate behavior.*

Friendly, cheerful Mr. Miller with those busy-bee eyes. I was glad now that the tuna fish and the Velveeta cheese were on top of the basket, not the junk. I looked down at what he had in his basket — spaghetti, some yellow detergent, and two six packs of beer. His basket didn't look that healthy.

"Is that Kevin?" he said, sticking out his hand. "Hello, Kevin. I'm Milo Miller. So this is where we finally meet. Did Billy tell you I was at the house?"

They stood there talking together. "How's the job going?" Miller said. "You're going to school, too. I bet you're busy."

Kevin straightened up his shoulders, then adjusted his glasses. It was Dr. Kevin. "Things are a little hectic, but I try to work with a plan and goals."

Miller liked that. He glowed. "Yes, a plan. We all need to be organized." He took out his pad. "I'm never without this. Give me your work number, Kevin, just in case I have to reach you."

Chapter 15

Lori butted into me from behind. "Who are you looking for?" We were outside school.

"You." Half true. I was waiting for her, but I'd been hoping to see Margaret Geri. I'd been over to the CYO a couple of times, but I still hadn't talked to her. Once I'd seen her in a dance exercise class, in a room full of girls prancing around in a circle.

"Here she comes."

I spun around, then realized I'd been had. "Very funny."

"Who is she?" Lori said.

"She who?"

"She Who, is that her name?" Lori glanced over

her shoulder. "You don't have to hang around. I've got things to do."

"I don't." This morning Kevin had told me the Rescue Mission was coming for Mom and Dad's bedroom furniture later in the day. "We have to keep Lori away," he said. Truth was, I didn't want to be around for that, either.

"Why don't we go get a soda?" I said. "My treat."

"I'm going to Maryanne's house."

I had to bite my tongue to keep from saying, *Isn't there anyone else in your life?* "When are you coming home?" I said.

"When I get there, I'll be there."

That was another thing I didn't like about the Maryanne connection. There was a bite to Lori now that had never been there before. That wasn't my sister, that was Maryanne talking.

"Where does Maryanne live? I'll meet you there and we'll go home together."

"What is this, a third degree? You don't have to worry about me."

She tied a kerchief under her chin. It framed her face, gave her a soft round look. There were times when I looked at Lori and saw Mom, looking out at me through Lori's eyes. When that happened, I couldn't be mad at her. "You look like Mom with that kerchief on, Lori."

I shouldn't have reminded her about Mom. It threw her off, really devastated her. Her left eye started twitching like mad.

"Hi, Baby." Maryanne came up with a lollipop in her mouth. She had her hair pulled back with a pink ribbon. She gave Lori a handful of lollipops.

"Hi, Mommy." Lori unwrapped a lollipop, the same color as Maryanne's.

I gave Maryanne a cool look and she gave me a cool look right back. "How come you're always with your brother? I see you come to school with him every day."

"Not every day."

"Every day I see you, you're with him."

"That's because Billy's afraid to cross the street by himself."

Maryanne snorted. "I thought so." She took Lori's hand. "You're walking over to my mother's place with me. Or do you have to go straight home with him?"

"I do what I want," Lori said, but she pulled me aside with a worried frown. "What are you going to do now, Billy?"

"Don't worry, I'll get somebody to cross me."

"No, will you feel bad going home alone? Do you want me to go home with you?"

"No, no, I've got things to do downtown, but I'm picking you up. Don't go home without me. Where do you live?" I asked Maryanne.

She rolled her eyes. "Corner of Washington and Seventy-third. Let's go, Lori."

"It's a beauty parlor," Lori said. "Gladys' Beauty Salon."

I went along with them for a while, not following them exactly, but going in the same general direction. On the corner, waiting for the light to change, I overheard Maryanne complaining about her family.

"My father says he's never going to live with my mother again. I wish he'd take my brother with him. Then my life would be perfect. The other day, he made me so mad I smashed a carton of milk on his head, and he went and squealed to my mother. My mother said I couldn't go out for a month, but I did, the next day."

It was after five when I met Lori at the beauty parlor. She came running out without her jacket on. "I'm not ready to go. You've got to come in first and meet Gladys, Maryanne's mother, and Jo and Betty." Her hair was fixed in a lot of thin braids and she was wearing an armful of silver bracelets. She waved them in my face. "Maryanne's. Aren't they beautiful?"

I was uncomfortable walking into the beauty parlor. I wanted to get my sister and leave, but Maryanne's mother started talking to me. It was embarrassing because I didn't like Maryanne. Her mother looked just like a big Maryanne. She had on a pink smock and wore her hair like Maryanne's, pulled back and tied with a ribbon. She sounded like Maryanne, too, brusque, a little rough, but there was something nice about her.

She lit a cigarette and offered to trim my hair. "I can't stand seeing boys with hair in their eyes."

"I don't have enough money with me."

"For Lori's brother, it's on the house. Do you want to sit down?" She took a scissors to my hair.

I liked her cutting my hair, the cigarette smoke and her warm hands on my head.

"Now you've got a face again," she said, stepping back.

97

Maryanne came outside with Lori and me, shaking her bracelets.

"Oh, I almost forgot." Lori started to remove the bracelets from her arm.

"They're yours," Maryanne said. "Keep them. How many times do I have to tell you?"

"Thanks," Lori said and hugged Maryanne.

"Bye-bye, Baby."

"Bye-bye, Mommy."

All the way to the bus stop, Lori talked Maryanne nonstop. The bracelets bothered me; they weren't cheap. They were real silver bracelets. Where did Maryanne come off giving them away? Was that her way of buying Lori's friendship? A handful of lollipops and then a bunch of bracelets?

It was dusk; people were hurrying home. It was hard not to feel sad. On top of a building I saw a wooden eagle with its wings spread and thought of the rope Dad had rigged up for Lori on the tree outside her bedroom window. She used to practice swinging on the rope, but she didn't use it anymore. She'd dropped her guitar, too.

On the bus, we sat in back, looking out the window. I glanced over at Lori. Those thin braids and silver bracelets made her look different, like another person — someone I didn't know anymore.

"Why'd you change your hair?" I said.

"Maryanne likes it."

"Are you going to wear it that way all the time?"

"Tomorrow Maryanne will give me another hairdo. She likes my hair. She likes to brush it and comb it."

"What's Maryanne to you?" I said. "What's that Mommy, Baby stuff?"

Lori closed her eyes. We hardly spoke the rest of the way home.

A white moving truck was double-parked in front of our house. All the lights were on and the doors were open. A man was pushing Mom and Dad's bed into the truck. "Look what they're doing." Lori ran ahead to the house. Upstairs, Mrs. Stein was watching out her window.

Kevin came out, carrying the headboard. "They came late," he said. "Hey, Lori, don't do that." She was snatching things up in the street, one of Mom's slippers, the cord to Dad's bathrobe. Then she ran into the house. I followed her. "They were supposed to be gone by now," I said.

She turned on me. "You knew. You knew! You sneak. That's why you came to Maryanne's. Pretending you wanted to go home with me."

A man carrying Dad's heavy winter overcoat and a pile of Mom's dresses passed us. I watched him throw the clothes in the back of the truck on top of other people's castoffs.

Afterward, I looked into Mom and Dad's room. The bed was gone, the curtains, the pictures on the wall. The room was bare, except for an oak bureau Kevin had bought at the Rescue Mission and a narrow mattress thrown down on the floor.

Chapter 16

I talked LJ into coming over to the CYO with me to work out with the weights. Now that I knew where I could see Margaret every day, I'd lost my nerve. I was building myself up — no pun intended — to saying something to her.

LJ really took to body building, a lot more than I did. He was always there ahead of me, hugging a steel weight to his chest and doing sit-ups on the slant board. Sweat poured off him. "You see that lard disappearing? How about it, cowboy, you working out or are you going to sit around on your horse all day?"

I tossed Dad's cowboy hat in the corner, stripped off my shirt, and began skipping rope, but my mind was upstairs with Margaret. She'd been saying hi, but she said that to everyone. I didn't want her to dismiss me as just anyone.

Next time maybe I'd put my hat on the counter. *Do you work here?* I'd say. (Now that was dumb. She was here all the time, wasn't she?) *You go to Schiller, don't you?* (That wasn't too bright, either.) *How do you like working here?* (Picking up dirty towels! Another brilliant question.)

Maybe she'd like Dad's hat. *Sure, try it on. It looks great on you, really. . . .* And then I'd say, *What time do you quit here? Maybe I'll walk home with you.* (No, don't say maybe. Say, I will walk home with you.)

Later when LJ and I came up from the weight room, he did all the talking. Not that he said that much. "Hi, Margaret!" He got even louder than normal around her. "How're you doing?"

It was late and getting dark when I got home, but Lori still wasn't in. What if she'd come in, found the house empty, and gone out again? I should have been home. I'd hung around the CYO too long. I should have called Maryanne, but instead I called Sam.

"Hello, Sam? Is Lori there? This is Billy."

"She's probably with Maryanne." Sam had this slow way of talking with lots of pauses. "Why don't you call her?"

"I'm not talking to Maryanne."

"Me, either," she said.

"Since when?"

There was a pause. "I'd rather not say."

"You two have a fight?" I could hear her breath rising and falling. "Where do you think they are?"

"Downtown, shopping. Maryanne loves shopping."

"And you don't?"

"Not with her."

"Lori doesn't have any money."

"Lori won't need money with Maryanne."

"What makes her so generous? Where does she get the bread? Her mother must really spoil her with money." But what I really thought was how easy it would be for someone to raid the cash register in the beauty parlor.

Lori came home late, her hair loose, wearing makeup and a pair of Mom's spiked heels. It made her look years older.

"Where have you been?"

"Wherever I've been, I've been." She snapped her fingers. "Where have you been?"

"Waiting for you."

"Check that out." She wobbled down the hall. "I've got to wash my hair."

"You washed your hair yesterday."

"Maryanne washes hers every day."

I was sick of hearing about Maryanne. The expert on everything. I didn't even want to mention her name again. "What do you want for supper?"

"Food bores me."

"Meaning you ate already. Maryanne's?"

"Why do you keep saying Maryanne? I was at Sam's house. Her mother made lasagne for me and we had peach cobbler for dessert."

"Lori, I just talked to Sam. You weren't at her house."

Lori's eye started to twitch. "Why are you calling

my friends about me? I don't want you spying on me."

"What were you and Maryanne doing? How come Sam doesn't like her?"

"Sam's afraid of her own shadow." Lori blinked at me. "Don't ever say anything about Maryanne to me! She's my best friend. She at least knows what day this is."

"Tuesday, what's the big deal?"

"You don't know, do you?"

"What?"

"Forget it. You don't know anything." She went to her room and slammed the door.

I went outside. What was that all about? In the distance I heard sirens and the steady roar of traffic. Windows were lit up. Families were home eating and watching TV. I wanted Mom and Dad here — now — where they belonged. They had no business running out on us. Being parents was their job, not mine.

When I came in, there was a light under Lori's door. The kitchen had been cleaned up, the dishes done, and everything put away. There was a piece of paper propped up on the kitchen table. It was a page from the calendar, the month of March, with a big red circle around the date. I picked it up. I still didn't get it. Why a red circle? And then I knew — Mom always red-circled our birthdays on the calendar. Today was Lori's birthday.

I knocked on Lori's door. "What?" she said. "Who is it?"

"Happy birthday, Lori," I said through the door.

"Shut up. I don't want your lousy greetings."

"I'm sorry I forgot."

"Shut up, Billy! It's too late. My friend remembered my birthday. My brothers forgot it." Then the light went off in her room.

Chapter 17

The next morning, Lori left for school without talking to me. "I'm sorry about your birthday, Lor."

What a look she gave me! Hurt. Mom's face when I'd disappointed her. Then Lori's eyes veiled over and there was nothing.

That afternoon when I came home from school, I told Kevin about forgetting Lori's birthday.

"How come you forgot?" he said.

"Same reason you did."

"You're closer to her."

"You're supposed to be older and wiser." The usual biting at each other.

"Come on, stop the bull. Let's get her something."

We took the car. This was an emergency. In a drugstore we bought her some English soap in a fancy box and a combination checkers and chess game. Then we went home and fixed up a bunch of devil's food cupcakes with a lit candle in each one.

"Surprise!" Kevin said when Lori walked in. "Happy birthday, a day late, happy birthday, dear Lori. . . ."

Lori sniffed the soap and fingered the checkers game. She ate a couple of the cupcakes. I thought she loosened up with Kevin. With me, too. Lori's not the unforgiving sort. Of course it wasn't my birthday, so it was easy for me to say. But then in the next couple of days I saw that things were definitely not the same. Lori wasn't talking to me. It wasn't my imagination. If I talked to her first, she'd answer and then only yes . . . no . . . maybe. . . .

I noticed other little things, like us not taking the bus to school together, or if we did, Lori always managing to find a place apart from me. And if we were in the same room together, she'd stiffen, draw herself up, and catch her breath, as if she couldn't stand to breathe the air I breathed.

Did I like it? No, I didn't like it, but I didn't know what to do about it. It's not easy to keep trying with someone who freezes you out.

Kevin had hardly returned from Boston when he started talking about going back again. He held out for two weeks and then he was off.

"What about the job?" I said. Kevin had said, himself, he couldn't afford to take any more time off because his boss was beginning to complain.

"Don't worry," he said cheerfully, "I'm not going to lose any time. I'm going to go straight from work Friday night, take the midnight bus. I'll sleep on the bus so I'll have all of Saturday and Sunday with Kathy. I'll be home Monday afternoon in time to go to work. See you, kids." He was happy. It was the Boston connection. Happy to be away from us.

"You better let me have the car keys," I said, "in case there's an emergency."

"There's no emergency. What emergency?"

It was Margaret, but I couldn't tell him that. I still hadn't said anything to her. That's why I fixed on the car. The Mercedes would be something to talk about. I'd park outside the CYO and when Margaret came out I'd give her a friendly honk.

"Is this *your* car?" she'd say.

I couldn't make my mind up if I should be sitting in the driver's seat or standing outside, maybe leaning against the fender or wiping the dust off the hood. "Would you like to go for a drive?"

It could all start with that — the drive, talk, etc., etc.

I followed Kevin to his room. "Leave me the keys, Kevin, or we're going to get a bunch of tickets."

"I'm going to leave the car at the bus station parking lot."

That was the pits. "Kevin, you're just asking for the car to be ripped off. They're going to tear the wheels right off her. Don't you worry about it at all?"

"I'd be a lot more worried knowing you're driving it."

"I'm a better driver than you," I said.

"That's why I'm not driving to Boston."

Kevin was trying to make me crazy. "It's not good for a car to sit. The wheels go flat on the bottom."

"That's a good one," Kevin said cheerfully. "That's an argument I haven't heard lately." He gave me money for groceries, and Kathy's number in case anything happened. "You've got the Steins upstairs and Steve and Holly. You'll be all right, don't look so worried. Buy toilet paper," he said, pulling on his knapsack.

"Look," I said desperately, "the reason I need the car is there's a girl. I'd like to show her the Mercedes sometime. She's interested in foreign cars."

"Oh, a girl! Interested in foreign cars! Now I understand you."

"Anything wrong with that?"

"At your age, not a thing. But if it's all right with you I'd rather you didn't do it in the Mercedes. Take her on the bus."

I didn't want to get excited. Keep it simple and plain and restrain the urge to strangle Kevin. "I just want to use it on this one occasion." That was reasonable, but sarcasm was unavoidable. "Considering that the car is mine as much as yours, I don't think that's too unfair."

"Look, I'm in a good mood and I want to stay that way." He slapped me on the cheek a couple of times. "I'll see you in a couple of days. Keep things together here."

It was a long, long weekend. Lori was in and out, but even when she was in she avoided me. Holly and

Steve were away, so was LJ, and Margaret didn't work weekends. I worked a little on the upstairs apartment and hung out with the Steins, watching Mrs. Stein upholstering a chair. It was cozy, the shades drawn, Mr. Stein asleep on the couch, and no sound except the tap of Mrs. Stein's upholstery hammer. Sometimes she sold a piece and made a little money. Mostly the furniture jammed their apartment.

I ate supper with them, too, boiled beef and potatoes and an apple cake Mrs. Stein had made fresh that morning.

"Where's Lori?" she kept asking. "I made supper for her, too. Why don't you call up her friends and see where she is?" Once Mrs. Stein got on a topic she didn't get off it. "How can a child stay away so long from the house? Your brother went away yesterday?" She put another piece of cake on my plate. "The poor boy misses his girl friend, so he goes away. Meanwhile, who's looking after these other two children? What do you think of that, Nate?"

Mr. Stein mashed his potatoes, then added salt and pepper. "I think it stinks, but who's asking us. You only get one set of parents in this world, and a lot don't even have that."

"I worry about these children. If I was twenty years younger I'd take the job myself. You know they don't eat the way they should. Don't shake your head, Billy. I know you're staying up too late. I hear you down there at night. Who's to blame you? No one there to tell you to go to bed. What kind of way is that to grow up? Look at the circles under his eyes, Nate."

"Cut it out, Lily. You're just making the kid feel rotten." Mr. Stein winked at me. "These kids are all right. It's tough right now, but they'll survive. They're not the first ones that had to grow up by themselves. It's going to make them more independent, self-reliant."

I cleared my plate. It was the one thing I didn't like about going up to the Steins. They were so worried about us. Didn't they have anything else to talk about but us?

Sunday morning I was asleep on the couch when the phone rang.

"Hello! Is your father home?"

"What?"

"This is Jerry Walker from the Y. Is this Joe's son?"

"What?" I couldn't breathe, my throat was so tight.

"Let me talk to your dad. Is he home?"

"No."

"Okay, just tell him if he wants to play tennis some Sunday morning, Jerry Walker is back in action. Back and raring to go. Tell him I have a court if he wants to play next Sunday. All he's got to bring are his sneakers and his jock strap. He has my number."

He hung up. I was in a hot sweat. I got back on the couch, but then I got right off again.

"Who was that?" Lori said, coming into the room. She was dressed and brushing her hair.

I pushed the phone out of sight. "A wrong number. Where are you going?"

"No place."

"Let's do something together." It was Sunday, a

110

day when the family was supposed to be together. I didn't want to be alone. "We could go to the movies later."

"I'm going out. I have something to do."

It turned out to be another long day. I watched a lot of television. Lori still hadn't come back that night when Kevin called. "How's Lori doing?" he said.

"Okay." Was that why he'd called? I didn't say that she still wasn't in.

"I'm going to have to stay one more day," Kevin said.

"You're not coming home?" I couldn't keep the disappointment from my voice.

"Did I say I wasn't coming? I'm coming, but one day late. I want you to call my job first thing tomorrow morning. Tell them I'll be in Tuesday. Is it snowing there?"

"No!"

"It's really coming down here. A freak storm. I don't think the buses are going to be running tomorrow."

When Lori came in, I told her Kevin wasn't coming home until tomorrow. "So?" she said, brushing past me. "They're having too much fun."

I called Kevin's job Monday morning before I left for school. The line was busy and I couldn't get to a phone until lunchtime.

"Kevin's not coming in today?" the man said. "What else is new?"

"I tried to get you first thing this morning. Is it going to be a problem?"

111

"No problem at all. I'll just hire somebody else."

Was he joking? "He'll definitely be there tomorrow."

"Tell him not to bother. I need somebody steady I can depend on. Every time he misses I've got to scrounge up an extra to cover his job. I'm sick of his excuses."

"He hasn't missed that much."

"What are you, his lawyer? He's missed."

"He needs the job. He's got a family!"

"Yes, so does everyone. Tell your brother he's got a week's pay waiting for him." And he hung up.

Chapter 18

That afternoon, I talked to LJ by the lockers. "I need a job." Maybe when I gave Kevin the bad news, I'd give him some good news, too. LJ thought I ought to check with the guidance office. "They list jobs."

"Donkey work," Eugene Connors said.

"That's right up his alley," LJ said. "Did you hear about the sweet potato who got brain damage?"

"You mean the one where the doctor says he's going to be a vegetable for the rest of his life?"

"Why do you always ruin a good joke, Connors?"

After school I went to the guidance office. There were only a few jobs listed on the bulletin board. I copied one down for a delivery boy, but by the time I got to the store it was gone.

Instead of going home I went into a bunch of stores. Nobody wanted me. That was a shocker. I always thought when I needed a job I could get one. After that, I didn't want to go home. Instead I went over to the CYO.

"How'd you get this job?" I asked Margaret. It was the first thing I'd ever said to her. What a way to start! I'd always thought I'd start talking to her sometime when I was feeling great, not rotten.

"Why do you want to know?" she said. "I'm not quitting if that's what you mean."

"I'm not looking for your job."

"What do you want, then?"

"Anything, as long as it pays."

"That's a good principle to start with. The super might be looking for somebody to mop the hallways."

"Is he here now?"

"She. You have to catch her before five or on Saturday."

"Thanks," I said.

The super was on a ladder upstairs changing a fluorescent light. Her glasses hung on a black ribbon around her neck. "Job?" she said. She set the long light down. "What job? Who told you to ask?"

"I just thought I'd check. I'm looking for work. I'd be willing to do anything."

She looked down. "No, not right now, but leave your name with the girl at the basket room."

"What happened?" Margaret said when I came back.

"She told me to leave my name here."

Margaret got out a pad. "Okay. What is it?"

"Billy Keller."

"Hi, Billy, nice to meet you."

"Nice to meet you, Margaret," I said. "You want a Coke?"

"Can you afford it?"

I held up the twenty-dollar bill Kevin had left me for groceries. When Kevin came home, he was going to kill me, anyway. What could I say in my defense? I should have called his job earlier, the way he'd told me to. Then the man wouldn't have had any excuse to fire Kevin.

I handed Margaret the drink. Kevin loved that job. It had taken him a long time to find it. He said working on an ambulance was the best possible job he could have had.

The phone rang. "Yes," Margaret said. She touched her lip. "You said you'd pick me up. No, that's okay!" She hung up, then stuck out her tongue at the phone. "That creep. He was supposed to give me a ride and he can't make it. Look at these heels. How am I supposed to walk home?"

The moment I'd been waiting for — Margaret needed a ride and I had nothing to offer.

Some girls came for nets and volleyballs. Margaret was busy. "I'll walk you home later," I said. "I mean, is it okay if I walk with you?"

"Sure, I'll get a leash, and you can follow me everywhere." She laughed, her mouth open. "Where's your friend?" She pulled a small pair of scissors from the drawer and cut a thread off her sleeve. "Big Stuff,

115

the one who comes in with you all the time? I don't see him hanging around the way you do."

I put my hand on hers. I must have been feverish. Everything was in such a mess. My hand found her wrist. Somebody else's hand, not mine.

"You're a fresh kid, do you know that? Don't you realize I'm a lot older than you?" She laughed.

"Age doesn't matter." How did people talk to each other? The corner of her mouth turned up like a paper curling. I picked up the scissors, touched the point. I wanted to impress Margaret, do something she couldn't laugh off, show her I wasn't just a dopey kid.

"Feelings matter," I said. "It's what you do that counts." That's what Kevin would tell me. *Good intentions won't buy you a ticket to Podunk. Why didn't you keep calling that phone number until the line was free?* I bounced the point of the scissors on my skin like a dart. Bounced . . . bounced them. . . .

"What did you do?" Margaret said. "Did you see what you just did?"

I looked down. I'd stuck the point of the scissors into my arm. Blood welled up under the skin.

Margaret pressed a towel down on my arm. My blood was on her fingers. "Why did you do that?" she said.

"I don't know. . . ."

"What are you, one of those kids who likes to get hurt?"

"No, I don't know why I did it." I was dazed. Why had I done that? What was she going to think of me

116

now? I lifted the towel. The bleeding had stopped. Only a tiny mark remained. "Do you have a Band-Aid?"

I sat down in a corner and waited while Margaret worked. I looked at a magazine, but I didn't know what I was reading. I kept glancing down at my arm and then up at Margaret. My arm throbbed a little. It didn't hurt that much. A purple stain was spreading under the Band-Aid.

Later Margaret and I stood out on the sidewalk together. A drizzle made the streets shine. Margaret muttered about having to go home in her high heels. "I'll walk with you," I said.

"Why don't you mind your own business." But a moment later she took my arm and my hat. "Let's go." She put my hat on. "If I step into dog poop, it's going to be your neck."

We walked by the playground. What would happen if I leaned against her? Put my face close to hers? Brushed my lips across her cheek? My lips across her lips.

She'd say, Where'd you learn to kiss?

Bad? I haven't had a lot of practice.

Good for a beginner. Don't press so hard, wet your lips.

I'm not too good.

Don't talk so much. Kiss me more.

"I still don't understand why you did that to your arm," she said.

"We live over there," I said, changing the subject.

"Do you rent?"

"No."

"You one of them?"

"One of who?"

"Those smart people who come in from outside the neighborhood and buy old houses cheap and make the people move, then fix them up and sell them for a lot of money."

"We didn't do that."

"I was born in this neighborhood," Margaret said, "right around the corner from here at All Saints Hospital. This is where I've lived all my life. On Ninety-seventh Street and before that we lived on the two-thousand block of Dyer. Me and my mother."

"Just the two of you?"

"Yes. My mother's an angel. . . . What's your mother like?"

"My mother's dead. Both my parents are dead."

"Both your parents?" She looked at me with surprise.

"They died in an airplane crash."

"You're the one everyone was talking about. Why didn't you tell me? I didn't know that."

After that she was nicer to me. We cut across an open lot full of rubble and weedy grass. Margaret lived in a big, brightly lit housing project on the other side. She put a hand on my shoulder. "Do you think about your parents a lot?"

"Yes." We stopped in the middle of the lot. She turned and kissed me, a sympathy kiss, a peck on the cheek. Then we kissed on the mouth. It made everything that had happened disappear from my mind.

Across the street from her building, she gave me my hat. "Now you think you can find your way home alone? That's a good boy."

I turned back across the lot. I was thinking about how much I liked Margaret — and then I started thinking about Kevin again.

Chapter 19

That all-American rat at American Ambulance was out to get me. He couldn't stand it that I was in college. Sarcastic smart ass. Always calling me doctor." Kevin threw down his knapsack. He'd just come home from Boston. "He was just looking for an excuse to get rid of me."

"Can't you go to the boss and tell him?" I said, relieved he wasn't blaming me.

"No way, it's his son. His father put that big ape in charge of everything. Anything his son does is all right with him." Kevin emptied his knapsack out on the floor. "Here. This is for you." He handed me a T-shirt printed with MY BROTHER WENT TO BOSTON AND THIS IS WHAT HE BROUGHT ME BACK. "Where's

Lori? I got one for her, too." He sat back on his heels and looked at the ceiling. "Do you know how much I want to go out looking for a job again?"

I started worrying, because that's what I did best. With Kevin out of work, where was the money going to come from? Mom and Dad had both worked and they never had enough. They were always worrying about money. Every month there were "musts" and "put offs." The mortgage was a "must" and the car payment and the electric bill. Clothes were a "put off" and meat every day. But that never made me feel poor the way I felt poor now.

What bothered me was that Kevin wasn't getting out there and looking. Not the day he came home — I didn't expect that — but the next day, and the next day, and the next day. He went to his classes and the library, but then he was home. First he said the weather was too bad, then he got a cold. He always had a cold when he came back from Boston. The weekend came and all he was saying was he'd never find a job as good as the one at the ambulance service.

"You just have to keep looking," I said. "Something's going to turn up."

"You look and see what it's like."

"I am," I said. "I have been looking."

"It's a meat market out there. You walk in and they look at you like you're a side of beef."

I went outside and washed the Mercedes, worried about what we were going to do if Kevin didn't find a job. Were we going back to Aunt Joan and Uncle Paul for another loan? How long could we do that?

121

"Nice wash job," a man walking by said.

What happened next was totally unexpected. "Want your car washed?" I asked, and I had a job.

It took me half an hour, and then his neighbor asked me to wash her car. I went home after that to tell Kevin there was money to be made washing cars. He was outside throwing a Frisbee with Steve. Holly was sitting on the stoop looking at the paper. "How's it going, Billy?"

"Good," I said. "Hey, Kevin."

He waved to me, then went running down the block after the Frisbee. I sat down next to Holly and told her about the car-washing business. "I think I've got the perfect part-time job."

"You can wash our car," she said.

"I wouldn't charge you."

She nudged me. "Some businessman."

That week Kevin went out looking for work a couple times. I was washing cars every day. It was money, but not that much. "Lunch money," Kevin said. He could have gotten on the extra list with a taxi company, but he turned them down. "I'd have to sit by the phone twenty-four hours a day. My life wouldn't be my own."

Then he decided he was going to work on the up-stairs apartment. "You're never going to get it finished alone. What have you done all month besides wash cars? I want to finish the apartment and rent it out. Then we'll have three rentals. I won't even have to have a full-time job. I can work part-time and go to school more. Two weeks is what I give us to finish the whole job. I'll be on it full-time and you work

122

when you come home from school. No more car washing."

Working with Kevin was the pits. I'd come home from school and he'd be waiting for me. I liked to have something to eat before I went upstairs, but he didn't give me time to sit down. "Come on, come on, how long are you going to eat? Bring that slop up with you. I want to talk to you about these cabinets." He was a demon once he got going. He didn't want to stop for anything. One night he didn't stop at all. "I'm going to work right through until this kitchen is finished. Sleep is just a state of mind."

At midnight, I lay down on the floor and went to sleep. He was still working. But things were getting done; the living room was finished, the bedroom, and all we had left was the kitchen and the bathroom.

In one way, though, it was great. When it came to the work, we were equals. In fact, in some things I knew more than he did, not that he admitted it, but I sure wasn't his helper on the job. He didn't know anything about electricity and I'd picked up enough from Dad so I could wire the switches without electrocuting myself. "That's your department," Kevin said. He didn't want anything to do with wires.

He wasn't always a slave driver. There were moments when it was really good to be together. Odd moments when we sent out for food and Lori drifted in, and we all sat around with the TV on, eating greasy chicken takeouts and making cracks at the commercials or playing games. We got into a bone-throwing contest one night, seeing who could pitch the most gnawed bones through the open skylight.

Kevin's "intensive" two weeks came and passed and the apartment still wasn't done. He began to get a little frantic. We were just about out of money and he was going to have to go back to Uncle Paul again. He was running from room to room, doing a little in the living room, then running to the bedroom and working on the closet, then back to the kitchen.

One day he said, "Let's rent it."

"You can't rent a place that looks like this."

"Get the toilet and the sinks working and somebody will grab it. At least I'll know the place is rented and money is coming in. We'll finish the work afterward."

Saturday night I was on the plumbing. It was after midnight when I made the last connections under the kitchen sink. Everything was hooked up and ready to test.

"No leaks?" Kevin said. "Everything's tight?"

"Okay," I said, "turn on the water."

Maybe I sounded a little more competent than I felt. It was just too satisfying to know more than Kevin. But then I went through all the connections again — the two sinks, the toilet, and the tub. It was two in the morning by then and I was so bleary I was seeing double.

Kevin went down to the cellar to turn on the main. I stood watching the toilet tank fill up. I turned on the faucets all over the apartment and let the shower run. Kevin came back up and danced me around the living room. That was more than the Steins could take. Mr. Stein came struggling up the stairs and said they couldn't sleep. "We're all done. We just finished," Kevin said. We rushed around turning off all the faucets and went downstairs.

A couple of hours later Mr. Stein was at our door. I never heard him. Kevin dragged me out of bed. The Steins' apartment was flooded. Water was dripping through the ceiling.

Sunday morning we had to find a plumber. What a mess. The ceiling in the Steins' apartment had to be completely replaced. By that time, we owed so much money Kevin wouldn't even talk to me.

Chapter 20

After the flood, Kevin stopped working upstairs. Doors still had to be hung and closet shelves put up, but the worst of it was the kitchen where the water had buckled the floor and ruined everything. The vinyl and plywood had to be replaced, but we didn't have the money to pay for it. Nothing was said. Kevin didn't blame me, not a word of blame, but some things don't have to be said. I blamed myself for what had happened and that was worse than anything else.

I'd pull up a corner of the vinyl and work for five minutes, then go up on the roof and worry about Miller coming around. You kids are doing a great job at living, he'd say. And what was I going to say?

Everything's great? The apartment upstairs was a mess, my brother had no job, and the three of us weren't talking to each other.

On sunny days, I picked up some car-washing jobs. Sam walked by one day when I was on Ninety-first Street, washing a car. "Hi, Billy!" I held up a dripping sponge just to remind her I hadn't forgotten the water fight. "What're you doing?" she said.

"Studying for my exams."

She blushed. "Oh, that was dumb of me."

"Not at all," I said. "Easy mistake to make."

"Oh," she said, "I knew what you were doing. It was just something to say."

"Want to help me?"

She stuck around and helped me finish drying the car. "Why don't you come around the house anymore?" I said.

"I'm still Lori's friend," she said, "but Maryanne told Lori not to be friends with me."

"That doesn't sound like Lori." I emptied the water in the gutter and wrung out the sponges. I said it, but did I really know what sounded like Lori anymore? "What makes Maryanne so powerful?"

"She's — oh, never mind. I don't like talking about Maryanne. Ask your sister." She handed me the towel and left.

"Thanks a lot, Sam," I called after her. I'd been thinking Lori had one good friend and one bad one. There was a balance there. But now it was Lori and Maryanne, period, and that was bad. Were they smoking dope? Maybe it was liquor or boys, or both. I remembered that night — that night before the phone rang — when I'd come looking for Lori at the CYO and we'd raced home. She wasn't like that anymore.

After I collected my money, I went over to the CYO and walked back and forth past the building.

Go in, I told myself. What can she do to you? Be your own charming self. *Hello, stranger. I've missed you.*

Hello yourself! I've missed you, too.

Then I'd sniffle a little. *I had a cold.*

How's your arm? I was a little worried you'd get an infection.

Next time I do that, I'll sterilize the scissors. . . . What time are you getting off? I'll walk you home. No, better still: *What time are you getting off? I have my car. I'll drive you home.*

It had been nearly a month since I'd stabbed myself and I still didn't have the nerve to face Margaret.

It started raining on the way home, a spring rain that made me think of Delmar and trout fishing with my friend Lamby. In the distance, thunder echoed over the rooftops.

At home I pulled off my wet shirt. Kevin was on his way out. "Better take the car," I said, "it's raining."

"The bus is on the corner."

"Leave me the keys and I'll park it nearer the house." Kevin still hadn't fallen for that ploy, but I tried anyway. If I could get my hands on the keys I could be at the CYO before Margaret quit. What better way to start talking to her again than by giving her a ride home on a rainy night.

Kevin slipped a couple of books into his knapsack. "If Kathy calls take the message."

"The car?"

"You can forget about the car."

There was something about the way he said it. I caught his arm. "Did you do something to the Mercedes?" I followed him into the hall. "Were you in an accident? Where'd you park it?"

"Billy. . . ." He opened the door, looked up at the sky. "You and that car. I'm afraid to tell you this, you're such a fanatic."

"What did you do to the Mercedes?"

He zipped up his jacket. "I sold it," he said.

"You sold the Mercedes! When?"

"Yesterday. It had to be done."

I looked at him, searched his face. "You sold her?"

"You make it sound like slavery. It's a car. It's sold. I told Lori. We needed the money. I'm sorry — I really am, Billy — but it's gone." He walked out.

"Kevin, wait." I ran after him, caught him at the bus stop.

"You haven't got your shirt on." He was getting on the bus. "Go home before you get sick."

I ran after the bus like a madman, then around the block, looking for the Mercedes. Dad had left me in charge of the car. He'd left me in charge, not Kevin.

When I got back to the house, Lori was home. "Lori, what did Kevin say to you about the car?"

She winced, then put her hand to her face. "What are you yelling for? I've got a headache, and you're making it worse."

"Kevin sold the Mercedes. Dad's car — our car.

He didn't ask us. Did he ask you? Would you have given your permission?"

She shook her head.

"Damn right, you wouldn't. The Mercedes is not for sale. It's ours — all of us — our family's. Damn that Kevin."

Kevin came home early. He had a carton of barbecued chicken wings that he put down on the coffee table. "I'm glad you're up. I want to talk to you. Where's Lori?"

"Asleep." I pushed my books away. "I want to talk to you, too."

"Help yourself to some wings." I just looked at him. No good, Kevin. You're not bribing me with a couple of chicken wings. "Kevin, we've got to get the Mercedes back. We can do it first thing tomorrow morning."

"Can't be done, Billy. I told you, the Mercedes is sold."

"We can," I said. "Don't say we can't. We can if we want to."

"Billy, you just aren't facing facts."

"Kevin!" If he were a car, he'd be a lemon, a piece of junk. If he were a car, I'd puncture all four of his tires, then kick out his windows, pull his wheels, yank his head, then flatten him and sell him for scrap to the junkyard.

I was furious, but I was ready to beg, too. "There are some things you can't replace no matter how much money you have. It was the last thing of Dad's we had."

"I know, I know, I know." He slapped himself on

the chest. "Do you think I liked doing it? I know how you feel, so will you please shut up."

I was trembling. I grabbed his shirt. I knew if I hit him I was going to be killed. I'd never beaten Kevin in a fight. I was asking for destruction, but I was so mad that for a moment it was a contest. I pulled him around, threw him off balance, but he was stronger than I was. He pushed me back, playing with me, the way we'd always fought. He'd let me try to hit him — *Go on hit me.* He'd catch my punches with his arms and shoulders, then grab my hands and tie me up. *Had enough?* He played with me the way you do with a kid.

He thought it was that kind of fight again. "Okay, got that out of your system?"

I went limp and he let up. I punched him hard in the stomach, then in the face. I went wild. I saw the hurt and surprise, and then the rage, on his face. He threw me back, jumped on me, pinned my arms to the floor. He slapped me left and right, one cheek and then the other, as hard as he could.

"How's that feel? Now you know how it feels to be on the receiving end." *Slap.* "You're no exception to the rule." *Slap.* "You've got to learn you can't have everything you want in this life." *Slap.* "Whining about the car. Come home, Kevin," he mimicked me. "Why aren't you home? Why aren't you working?" *Slap.* "Grow up and smell the grass. Everything isn't yours because you're Billy Keller.

"There are some things you can't have, things you've got to bust your hump to get, things you're never going to have. You can't be looking to me all the time, then blaming me because you can't have what you want. Depend on yourself for a change, you crybaby. I came home. What are you doing? Crapping around upstairs. Everything is Kevin, Kevin, Kevin. Where's the money, where's the job, what are we going to do? What am I, your daddy and your mommy? Why do I have to be the good guy? I'm not that good. You want to know the truth, I don't give a damn about you half the time."

Lori pulled Kevin off me, screaming at him. "Let go, Kevin! Kevin!"

He released me. I got up, tucked my shirt in. My eyes stung. I ran my tongue around the inside of my mouth, tasted blood. I walked around him with my head cocked, like I was going to start fighting again, round and round. *Not afraid of you, Kevin. Not impressed.* I closed my mind to his words. Then I went to my room and shut the door.

Lori followed me. "Billy?" She opened the door. "Are you all right?"

"Leave me alone."

"You want me to get you something?"

"No. Just get out."

Chapter 21

A light shining in my face woke me up. I covered my eyes, turned away. I didn't want to wake up. My whole head ached. My face felt hot, swollen, like it didn't belong to me.

"Billy." It was Kevin.

I sat up. He leaned over the bed, shining a flashlight into my face.

I scrambled over to the other side of the bed. Was he back to finish the job? "Get that light out of my face! What are you doing here? What time is it?"

"Let me see you."

I swung wildly at him.

He kept shining the light in my face. "God, did I

do that? Your cheek is lacerated. Does it burn? And your eye looks awful."

"Your own tender touch, Doctor."

"I'm going to get something for it." He ran out. Gingerly, I felt along my face. My cheek was puffed up, hot, lumpy. Nothing was where it belonged.

Kevin returned with a cold cloth. I pushed his hand away. "It will only sting for a minute. It's going to make it feel better."

"Hands off."

"Billy, I'm not going to hurt you."

"Don't touch me!" I grabbed the cloth. "I'll do it myself."

Kevin sat down next to me. "Does it hurt?"

"No, it feels wonderful."

He sat there, telling me how bad he felt. "I can't believe I did that to you. I don't believe it." He kept flashing the light on my face. "It makes me sick to see it. I don't beat up my brother. Isn't that right? I never did this to you before. Isn't that right? I don't know what to say, Billy."

"Say you're sorry for starters, you pig."

"I am sorry, Billy."

"Who gives a damn."

What did he think, all he had to do was act concerned and sympathetic and everything would be the way it was before? My face ached like a toothache. I didn't have any forgiveness in me. I hadn't forgotten what he said. I threw down the cloth. "Get out of my room."

In the morning I couldn't get my right eye open.

134

I lifted it with my finger, but when I let go, it shut again. I wasn't going to school with that. I felt my way to the bathroom. Lori's door was closed. Maybe she wasn't going to school, either.

"How do you feel this morning?" Kevin said in the kitchen.

I moved around to the other side of the table. "Get away from me."

"Billy, you're not still mad at me, are you? I'm sorry, you don't know how sorry I am. I couldn't sleep last night."

"I really feel sorry for you."

"Let me see your eye. Can you see out of it?"

"Right through my eyelid. One eye is all I need to see you, brother. You think you can talk your way out of anything."

"Billy, I'm *sorry*."

"You're lying. Tell the truth, Kevin. You had a great time beating me up. It was fun, wasn't it? You couldn't hit me fast enough. Knock some sense into that dumb kid. I saw the shine in your eyes. You couldn't get the words out fast enough, you were so eager to tell me what was wrong with me. Don't shake your head. You liked hitting me. You've been wanting to hit me for a long time."

It shut him up. He sat down at the table, started folding and refolding a napkin.

I got the milk out of the refrigerator and stood there with the door open, drinking it. *Just say something, Kevin, and you get this quart of milk right in your face.*

He started banging pots around. "I know you don't

believe me, Billy. I sound like a moron, apologizing and saying the same thing over and over again. I am sorry. That's the truth." He sat down. "I know it isn't good enough. I wasn't the one who was beat up. I don't blame you for not believing me. How can I tell you how bad I feel?"

"Don't try." I bit into an orange. It stung the inside of my mouth and I spit it out in the sink.

"I feel bad, Billy. Bad! I never in my life thought I'd do anything like this. It's been building up. I see it now. I've been blaming you from the beginning, getting madder and madder at you for everything that's gone wrong."

"No kidding." I soaked bread in a bowl of milk and swallowed it gingerly.

"Things haven't been good between us for a long time."

"It was good when you first came home."

"No, it was never good. Maybe you felt good, but me — I was covering up from the beginning. I thought I was a real hero when I came home. Mr. Good. Coming home to take care of you kids, sacrificing my future for the family. I was Mr. Terrific. All make-believe. All grandstand. Kathy tried to warn me."

He was so humble. I'd never seen Kevin act this way before, not my big-shot brother. "Okay, Kevin, okay, that's enough. I believe you."

He leaned forward, his face was blurry, out of focus. "Billy, I feel I haven't acted right to you, not just the fight — I haven't been honest with you." He started crying.

That really wrecked me. This was my brother, my big brother, the one who did everything right. "Kevin! I'm okay. My eye — yeah, it's okay. It isn't that bad." I reached over and caught his hand. "Come on, brother."

He grabbed my wrist, squeezed it hard.

We sat that way for a few minutes. Then Kevin got up and washed his face at the sink. "You want some of this bread and milk?" I said. "It sounds like cat food, but it's really good."

Chapter 22

I wore dark glasses in school because one side of my face looked like an oatmeal cookie. The glasses mostly hid it. "Who hit you?" LJ said.

I shrugged, ashamed to admit my brother had beaten me up. Besides, I didn't want to put Kevin down. Not now. A storm had come and passed, and the air between us was clear.

After school I stopped at the CYO. The dark glasses gave me courage. I felt hidden with them on. But Margaret saw right through them. "What happened to your face? Who beat you up?" She stopped to take care of a kid with wet hair, then came back to me. "Come here, let me see it." She pulled me into the light. "What are you, one of those kids who like to get hurt? What am I going to do with you? Don't you know when you see trouble you're supposed to go the other way?"

"I'm going to walk home with you," I said.

"I've got a ride tonight. Anyway, do I need you to protect me? I better take you home. You still haven't told me who did it to you."

"It doesn't matter. It wasn't all his fault. I was asking for it."

"You? You're a cupcake."

I hung around talking to her, helping her hand out baskets, then I went to check with the super again. "I've got you on my list," she said. After that I went home and did a little bit of work on the apartment. The job was basically on hold until we got some money. Kevin came in while I was making sandwiches for Lori and me. "One of those sandwiches for me? Guess what? I'm working."

"You got a job?"

"I took the taxi job." He bit into the sandwich. "No big deal, but it's a job."

"You're driving a cab. Someone's going to let you drive their cab. Good God, Kevin, don't go down any one-way streets, and don't be a cowboy. Devote yourself. You can be a good driver. Dad was. I am. Mom was. If you're a Keller, you're not hopeless."

"The dispatcher says I should get thirty hours. He's a real character."

"Who?" Lori said, walking in.

"This guy on the job. He's been around a million years. He says he's going to look out for me."

"You got a job?" Lori said. "Nobody told me."

He put his arm around her. "What'd you think, honey, I'd leave you in the lurch?"

She pulled away. "Where's my sandwich? You're supposed to make me a sandwich, Billy."

"I'm working as fast as I can. Kevin ate it."

She poured herself a glass of Kool-Aid. "I see you two have made up."

"That's right," Kevin said. "We're one big happy family again. Make me another sandwich, Billy."

"His eye looks terrible," Lori said.

"It's better, isn't it, Billy?" Kevin said.

I pulled it open. "Is there an eyeball in there, Lori?"

"You two make me sick." She took her sandwich and drink into the living room.

After school a couple of days later, LJ and I were standing outside the Pie Shop across from the school, sharing a slice of pineapple cheese pie. LJ had his arm around me, telling me rotten jokes. "Do you know the kind of girl Count Dracula likes?"

"No."

"The one who brings out the beast in him."

On the street a truck honked. I looked up and saw a yellow cab with Kevin at the wheel. "Did you see that, LJ?"

"What?"

"My brother driving a cab. Kevin!" I yelled and ran after him.

At the corner, the light turned red and I banged on the window, then jumped in the back. Kevin turned. "Where'd you pop in from?" He pulled the cab to the curb. He was wearing his black T-shirt, the silver pendant around his neck. Beside him he had a clipboard and a paperback book open on its face. Taped to the ashtray was an aluminum change holder. He looked like a cab driver.

"Cab?" A man said.

I jumped out and held the door open. "This way, sir." I ran around to Kevin's side and slapped the door. "Get to work, Kevin. Get moving."

Things were looking up again. We'd been down in the dumps. I sure had. For a while everything I touched seemed to go bad. I still woke up sometimes and thought, Would Kevin have lost his job if I'd called the guy at the ambulance service first thing that morning? And the apartment — that flood — it had been a national disaster. I was afraid to ask Kevin how much we owed Uncle Paul. And then the fight with Kevin — that had been the bottom.

I went downtown to Chigley's to buy some T-shirts. Mine were falling apart. I wasn't going to buy that many, just two or three — Celebration T-Shirts. I was on my way out of the store when I saw my sister and Maryanne at the cosmetic counter.

Maryanne was trying a lipstick and pointing to something in the display case. When the saleswoman looked down, Maryanne pocketed the lipstick, then moved on to another counter. You're seeing things, I told myself. Maryanne tied a scarf around her neck and showed it to Lori, then picked up a second scarf. Where was the first one? Palmed? Up her sleeve?

I came up behind them and took them each by an arm. It wasn't a thought. I was moving, walking them both out of the store. Not rushing, not running or making a commotion, but moving quickly down the aisles to the revolving glass doors. Afraid that any second a heavier hand would fall on me, an alarm would sound, and all the doors would slam shut.

Outside, Maryanne shook me off. "Get your paws off me. Who do you think you're grabbing?"

"Are you crazy? I saw what you did. Anybody could have seen you."

"Seen what?" Maryanne raised her shoulders, bluffed me out. "What are you talking about? Make sense. We were shopping. What's wrong with that?"

"Lori," I said, turning to my sister. "I don't care what she does. What were you doing in there? Do you know what she was doing?"

Maryanne shoved between us. "You don't have to listen to him. Don't let him bully you, Baby."

"Lori, you don't need her to talk for you."

"We were shopping," Lori said, looking at Maryanne.

"I don't believe you. I don't believe either of you. Let's see what's in your pockets," I said to Maryanne. "Open up!"

"Make me."

"I saw you take a lipstick and a scarf. What else did you take?" I was mad and I knew I was right, but I wasn't as certain as I sounded. What if I was wrong? Was I going to end up apologizing to Maryanne? "I saw something — "

"Saw what?" Maryanne said. "How long have you been spying on us? You don't trust anybody, do you?

Not even your own sister. Some family you've got, Lori."

I caught my sister's arm. "Lori, let's go someplace where we can talk by ourselves."

Maryanne took Lori's hand. "Come on, Lo. Come on, honey. Let's get away from here." The two of them walked away together.

Chapter 23

I was in the kitchen when Lori came in. Go slow, I warned myself. Listen, don't start in by shooting off your mouth. It doesn't have to be what you think it is.

"Hi, Lori."

No reply. She dug peanut butter from the jar with her finger.

"Lori, in Chigley's today, I saw Maryanne put something in her pocket. A lipstick. And then a scarf. Did you see her do it?"

She pushed past me and got out the bread and jelly.

"Maybe I'm wrong, but you were right there, Lori. Tell me, am I wrong? Maybe my eyes deceived me."

I wished they had. "When I pulled you and Maryanne out of the store I was scared. Maybe I didn't handle it the best way, jumping in and accusing Maryanne. Okay, give me the facts. I'll listen."

She took her sandwich to her room and locked the door.

I stood at her door. "Just promise me one thing. Say you won't go 'shopping' with Maryanne anymore. Lori — " I banged on the door. "You're going to talk to me, Lori. I'm going to stay here till we have this out. Don't tell me you don't know what I'm talking about, because you do."

She started playing her guitar, hitting the strings as hard and ugly as she could.

"Sooner or later you're going to have to talk to me. Or am I going to have to tell Kevin?" I was sorry as soon as I said it. What flashed through my mind was what Kevin had yelled when he was beating me up. *Leaning on me . . . leaning on me . . . I'm not your daddy and mommy. . . .* He was right. I did lean on him. I was always looking for Kevin in every situation. Well, not this time.

"Hey, Lori, when you get caught they're not going to look at Maryanne, you know. She's got a family. They're going to look at you, and then they're going to say, 'Who's this bright thirteen-year-old? Where's her family?' And then they're going to call Mr. Miller in and he's going to say we can't leave those kids alone together because they don't have the brains they were born with. What's Maryanne going to do for you then?"

I was trying to be the calm, understanding older

145

brother, but I didn't impress myself. I didn't have a lot of natural patience or much faith in my ability to convince her. I couldn't talk the way Dad could, on and on till you saw your mistake and were sick of hearing about it.

"Lori?" Silence. "Is that your answer? If that's the way you are, there's nothing more to say." I waited. "Lori, are you going to come out and talk or not?"

She came out but not to talk. I was in her way and she swung at me, punched me hard a couple of times. "You spy. You filthy liar, what did you follow us for? Don't say anything about Maryanne."

"I bet Sam doesn't go 'shopping' with Maryanne."

"Don't try to be smart, Billy. Don't use psychology on me." Her left eye twitched. "Nothing's ever going to break Maryanne and me apart. She means more to me than anybody."

"Including me and Kevin?"

"Yes, including you and Kevin." She went back into her room and locked the door again.

I was frying an egg the next morning when I heard a clatter in the hall. It was Mrs. Stein, bumping a chair down the stairs. "Oh, you're home, Billy. I was going to leave it outside your door. This chair is for you, for all three of you. It's a present."

It was the yellow chair she'd been working on. "It's what's called an occasional chair." She followed me into the apartment. "You can use it anywhere. It didn't take two yards of fabric. Sit in it. It's comfortable, isn't it? I think you should put it near the television."

146

I moved furniture around until Mrs. Stein was satisfied. "Yes, right there. When you get things right, they feel right. Enjoy."

I thought of her coming down the stairs, carrying the chair with those broken hands of hers. She didn't have to do that. She didn't have to do any of the nice things she did for us. It got to me in an emotional way, but after she left I still put everything back the way it had been. I didn't like things changed.

There was no place for the chair in my room or Kevin's room, either. Lori's room smelled of bubble gum and incense. All her clean laundry was on the bed and the dirty stuff on the floor. I buried the chair under a pile of clothes and pushed it into the corner.

Then, instead of leaving, I poked around her closet. I told myself I was looking for the chinning bar she wasn't using anymore. There was a knapsack on the shelf and a canteen. Behind it, all the way in back, was a small cardboard box. I pulled it down. I wasn't prepared for what I found. No, that's not true. In a part of my mind I knew. Ever since I entered the room and started looking, I had half expected this.

I dumped the box on the bed. Necklaces, silver and gold bracelets, earrings came spilling out, labels and price tags still on them. More jewelry, scarves, and lipsticks than anyone could ever use. There were even yo-yos still in their plastic seals.

I left everything on the bed and walked out. No covering up anymore. No more lies. Lori had lied right to my face. I never thought she would. Why not? We all lied. Didn't I? Telling myself I was Lori's

147

protective older brother. The truth was I didn't think about her, no more than I had to. I thought about Billy. Kevin was right about that, too.

I didn't know what hit me harder — knowing that Lori was stealing or feeling that I'd let her down. We were supposed to be helping each other, the older helping the younger. Hadn't I known, right down in my gut, what Maryanne was? I'd just let those silver bracelets she gave Lori slip right out of my mind.

For a long time I walked. It was a hot day. I found myself on a wide treeless boulevard in a strange neighborhood. In the distance everything was white and chalky with heat. I passed a liquor store with metal bars on the windows near a concrete overpass. Cars raced past overhead. A gang of men came rushing out of a bar, shouting and tearing at one another.

I stood there and watched. What were they doing? They were beating each other. Were they angry? Were they playing? Were they just doing it to have something to do? Did people do things for no reason, with no purpose?

Was that all life was? People running around like ants? There was meaning to ants. Everything they did had a purpose. What was the meaning of people?

I started walking again. What if I kept going and never turned back? Who would stop me? Who would care? Lori? *Yes, Billy was here today. I don't know where he is now.*

In the distance I saw the bus depot. Buses were announced, arrivals and departures. People streamed in and out of the doors. I went inside, stood in a corridor staring at a row of gray lockers. Each had a number and a keyhole like an eye. I reached into a locker, all the way in back. *Excellent, you just made a thorough investigation of an empty locker.* What was I looking for? What did I expect to find, a book waiting for me with the answers in back written upside down?

In a grocery store, I bought a carton of grapefruit juice and drank it in the playground near our house.

"What are you drinking?" Holly called from the street.

"Grapefruit juice."

She sat down on the swing next to me. "It's been a long time since I've been on one of these." She swung a little. "How's the apartment going? I want to come up and take a look before I get too pregnant to climb the stairs. Steve and I talked about taking it when it's done. I love the light up there and we could have a garden on the roof."

"It's going to be ready soon."

"That's good, so what's wrong, Billy?"

I pushed back on the swing. *Wrong? Nothing's wrong. Everything's wrong. Everything's a mess.* I swung past her. *We're broke . . . no money . . . and my sister —* And then afraid I was going to say something about Lori, I swung harder.

"Kevin was telling us the other night that once you finish the apartment you're going to be all right."

We're never going to be all right. . . . We made a mistake . . . it's my fault . . . I made it happen . . . it's my fault . . . my fear. . . . I stood up on the swing and

149

pumped hard. "Fear," I yelled. "Fear, fear, fear."

She looked up at me, laughing. "You're like a big bird, Billy."

The Keller family is no more. . . . It ended when that plane crashed. That's when it ended. . . . I pumped the swing up higher; the wind pushed in my face.

I was scared. Scared of what was in my head, scared of what I was thinking. I snapped the chains. I made the steel scream. *No . . . it'll never be the same again.*

Chapter 24

I smelled cigarette smoke the minute I walked into the house. "Lori? Kevin?" It was suppertime and getting dark out. In the kitchen there was a knife stuck in the peanut butter jar. "Lori?"

Mrs. Stein's yellow chair was in the hall outside Lori's room. The cardboard box — all the stuff I'd dumped on her bed — was gone. Doors were open everywhere, in the apartment, in the hall, upstairs. . . . Upstairs, the skylight was open, a ladder raised beneath it.

Lori was on the roof. When she saw me she went to the edge. In the dying light I saw every line of the rooftops, saw the wind lift her hair, saw the fine line of her neck . . . saw my sister falling. *Kevin. Mom and Dad. Stop her.*

Lori sat with her feet over the edge. "Lori," I said softly, "come on back."

She rolled over, let herself down over the side and balanced on a narrow gutter that ran just below the rooftop. I was afraid to say anything, afraid to move. Was it only a moment? It felt like forever. I crouched down, stretched my hand out toward her. She edged away from me.

Was she out of her mind? I was nearly crazy myself. There was nobody to help me, nobody to turn to. I started talking, just talking, saying anything. "How are you?" I thought if I said normal things to her maybe she'd act normal, too. "I've been looking for you. Are you hungry? I am. Come on down and we'll eat. I'd like a cream cheese and scallion sandwich. How's that strike you? You can have whatever you want. I'll make it. How about we make popcorn and play Monopoly. It's been a long time since we played. But maybe you'd rather play checkers. Whatever you want to do."

She watched me from the corner of her eyes. There was a guarded, clever look on her face.

"Remember how the two of us beat Kevin playing basketball? Maybe tomorrow, you and I will take Kevin on."

"He just plays around with us."

"No, Lori, he was playing all-out." I scooted a little closer. "Here, take my hand."

She sidestepped away from me. "What are you so worried about?" She let go with one hand. "Do you

152

think I could fly? If a person wanted to enough and let go and really believed, it would be like swimming. If someone threw you in the water and you couldn't swim, you'd swim, wouldn't you?"

"Lori."

She put her free hand to her hair. "Don't you love the wind?"

"Lori, I love you! I don't want to see you get hurt. Come on, Lori. Give me your hand. Please!"

She sighed and then put her arms over the top. I pounced on her, pulled her up, and dragged her over the roof. "Let me go!" she screamed at me. She fought me all the way downstairs and into the house. "Let go. You're always grabbing me. Did you think I was going to jump? Do you think I'm crazy? Leave me alone, Billy. Haven't you done enough?"

I didn't let go of her till we were in her room.

She sat on the bed, clutching the pillow. She was trembling and I was trembling and I couldn't catch my breath. I pulled Mrs. Stein's chair into the doorway and sat down facing her. I didn't care if I looked like a jailer to her. What if I hadn't come back?

I rubbed the arm of the chair. Her silence scared me. What was she thinking? What should I do? What should I say? "What do you think of this chair, Lor? Mrs. Stein gave it to us. Pretty nice, huh? She reupholstered it herself. Just took two yards of material. She wanted to put it in the living room — "

Lori swung the pillow against the bed. "Don't baby-talk me, Billy."

"Listen, Lori, I know you're down on yourself because of what happened with Maryanne. You probably think I blame you. I don't. We all make mistakes. That's all I make is mistakes, and Kevin does, too. You know if Mom and Dad were here none of this would have happened. You know that, don't you? Don't blame yourself. It's not your fault. I should never have let you be friends with Maryanne."

"It's got nothing to do with you! Who are you to be picking my friends? And besides, I can get into trouble by myself. I don't need your help. Or Kevin's, either. Don't shake your head, Billy. I know the way you and Kevin think about me." Her mouth twisted. "Pat her on the head and put her to bed. What a good little girl. I'm not good! I don't have to be good for you or Kevin or anyone else. You're not Mom and Dad. You're no better than I am."

"I never said I was." I tried to catch her eye. "Come on now, Lori."

"Come on now, Lori," she mimicked. "You're so superior, you and Kevin. You both think you can tell me anything or not tell me — whatever suits you. You think I'll always be your good little wimp." She drew a cigarette from her jacket pocket and lit it, squinting against the smoke.

"What are you trying to prove with that cigarette?"

"Nothing. And I don't need your advice, either." She took several puffs and blew the smoke at me.

I used to be able to talk to my sister, talk her around to anything. I used to think I understood her. Well, I thought a lot of things. Now I was afraid. There was something unpredictable in Lori that I didn't understand. Something impenetrable that

154

wouldn't listen, that didn't want to hear anything.

She opened the window. "What are you doing, Lor?"

"Just watch." She ground the cigarette out on the windowsill. "Why are you looking at me with your big blank face, Billy? Did you hear anything I said? Do you ever listen to me? Do you even know I'm alive?" Her voice trembled. "Stop looking at me. Stop it."

I put my hands on the arms of the chair. "Lori, calm down, will you?"

"No, I won't! What do you know? What makes you such an expert? You and Kevin, you're like two dogs. You love each other and then you hate each other, and then you love each other again. I can't stand it anymore. You don't know me . . . you don't care . . . you just don't care. . . ."

She stood there with her back to the wall, hands twisted together, her eyes squeezed shut, like the whole world was against her.

I started to go to her but the look she gave me kept me back. "Lori, you're wrong, you're wrong. I do care! But I'm not Mom and Dad. I'm just your brother. I'm not perfect."

"Tell me all about it." She slid down on the floor against the wall.

"Probably I'm making a mistake this minute, talking instead of listening. You're supposed to listen to people. Okay, I'm listening to you, Lori."

"You're just saying it because you're afraid of what I might do."

"I mean it, Lori." She cocked her head, looked at me disbelievingly. Too quick with the word. Kevin would have done it better. I kicked the rung of the chair. Stop calling Kevin all the time. Kevin's not here. You're the one who's here. You're the one who has to make sense. "What I mean is, you're my sister. I care about you. I worry about you."

"Sometimes you do, sometimes you don't. Most of the time you treat me like I was your pet goldfish. It's you and Kevin. The two of you are always figuring things out together. I don't count. I'm not a person to you. Just little Lori."

"Things aren't that great between Kevin and me."

"I know, he beat you up, but now you're friends again. He wouldn't even work on the apartment upstairs without you. Neither of you wanted me up there. You made me feel like I was always in the way."

"Not true."

She looked up at me. Her eyes were filling with tears. "I'm a person, too, Billy."

"I know you are."

"You don't act that way. You say it now, but you don't act it. You don't hear what I'm saying. Right now, I bet you don't hear what I'm saying. You hate it when Kevin acts so patronizing and bossy with you. Well, I hate it, too."

I felt stymied. What did she want? Everything I said she turned around. I tried to think. What would Mom and Dad do? Mom would get Lori right in her lap. She wouldn't talk so much. She'd hold Lori, pet her, rub her back, let Lori yell and scream till everything came out, all the tears, whatever was eating at her.

Hold her in my lap? Me? Then I thought, When she was on the roof I would have done anything. In a way, weren't we still on the roof?

"Lor — I've been thinking about Mom and Dad. . . ." This wasn't going to work. "You want to sit in my lap and talk?"

She looked up at me and made a disgusted face.

"I don't mean baby stuff," I said quickly. "It's just — that's what Mom would do, right? Her lap was the family conference center."

"When was the last time you sat on Mom's lap, Billy?"

"Uh — quite a while ago."

"I don't want to sit on your lap."

I squatted down next to her, my arm awkwardly across her shoulders. "Give me your hand, Lori." Her fingers knotted against me.

"Remember when were on the roof and I said I loved you?"

"No."

"I meant it, Lori."

She put her face against the wall. "I didn't want — " She shook her head. "You won't understand! I didn't want it to happen . . . I didn't, Billy! Stop laughing."

"I'm not laughing. I'm nervous. This whole thing is making me nervous."

"Is that my fault, too? Oh, never mind, I don't know what I'm saying. Maryanne said if I didn't steal that stuff, I couldn't be her friend."

"Why didn't you talk to Kevin or me?"

"You wouldn't have listened. You're hardly listening to me now!"

I clamped my fingers over my lips to show that I was listening and regretted it immediately. I was still playing games. I fell silent.

"Lonely. You don't know how lonely I am, Billy. Sometimes I feel there's nobody left in the world for me. Please don't say anything. Don't tell me you're lonely, too. You have Kevin. I don't have anyone."

I listened. I didn't have anything to say. "Lori — let's get in the chair." She let me pull her up and we squashed into the chair together.

Lori wiped her nose. "Maryanne despises everyone. Her teachers, all the other kids. Sam. Her parents, her brother. I'm the only one she likes. I'm the gutsy kid. Nobody else has the nerve we do."

"What about Sam?"

"I'm not that special to Sam. Maryanne — she really cares about me."

"She doesn't act like somebody who really cares."

"She cares! Don't you hear what I'm saying? She calls me every morning. She always knows when I feel bad. More than you, Billy. More than Kevin. She thinks about me, like Mom did. She braids my hair and buys me things."

"Buys?" I couldn't resist saying it. "Is that what it's called?"

"She didn't steal everything. She bought me things, presents."

Why was she still defending Maryanne? It was hard

for me to just sit and listen to her. Everything she said made me want to jump in and straighten her out. "Maryanne was never your friend, not your true friend."

"She was!" Lori exclaimed. "Why do you keep saying she wasn't? Don't you hear what I'm saying, Billy? I'm trying to explain what happened. I was lonely. I didn't have anyone."

I shut up and let her talk. After a while she got quiet, leaned against me. "I'm hungry," she said. "I want a toasted cheese and tomato sandwich with onions."

"Onions make your breath smell."

"That's what I want. I want to stink."

We were in the kitchen when Kevin came in. "Anybody home?" he yelled from the hall.

Lori grabbed my hand. "Don't say anything. Please, I'm scared to tell Kevin."

Kevin dumped his books on the table. "What are we eating?" He took the other half of Lori's sandwich. "Make a few more, Billy. Studying makes me hungry as a bear." He took the milk from the refrigerator. "What are you both watching me for?"

I looked at Lori. She shook her head, but a moment later she ran out and came back with the box. "Here," she said, handing it to Kevin. "Here."

"What's this?" He poked around, picked up a bracelet, then a lighter. "Where'd this stuff come from? This something from school? Where'd you get this stuff, Lori?"

"That's from Chigley's, that's from the Downtown,

the Downtown Store, that's — " She tripped over her words. She pointed to things — a bracelet, a ring, a scarf — saying where each one came from.

"Is this something you're doing for school?" He held up two lighters. "Comparison shopping? Who's paying for this?'

"I stole it," Lori said.

"Stole it?" He was smiling. "What kind of joke is this?"

"I stole it," she said again. "It's the truth. I was shoplifting. Maryanne and me. We stole it, Kevin, we stole it!"

"You, Lori?" Kevin said. "You?" He turned to me. "Where were you, Billy? Did you know this was going on?"

"Leave Billy out of this," Lori said.

"You want all the credit, is that the idea?" He turned on her. "Is this some kind of dare, some kind of crazy joke? Maryanne? Did she make you do it?"

"Nobody made me do it."

"She was lonely — " I started.

"Shut up, Billy."

"Why were you friends with a person like that? What would have happened if you got caught? They could put you in a detention home, send you away. They could do anything they want to you." He turned on me. "*Didn't you know your sister was stealing?*"

"*He* didn't steal," Lori screamed. "What are you worried about *him* for? I was the one. Me. Me, Kevin! You're so worried about yourself. They wouldn't do anything to you."

"You think I want to see my sister a jailbird?

160

Locked up? Made to live someplace she doesn't want to live?"

"You wouldn't care!"

He glared at her. "What the hell are you talking about?"

She started crying again, and it all came out, everything she'd told me about being lonely for Mom and Dad, and how Kevin and I didn't see what was in front of our eyes, and how Maryanne cared for her.

As she talked, I kept seeing Lori on the edge of the roof. How could it have gotten this bad and we didn't know anything about it? We were brothers and sister, living in the same house. Would Mom and Dad think we were doing such a great job of staying together? What was it worth? Kevin, half in, half out of school. Lori, so mixed up she did crazy things.

"I'm never going to steal again," she said. "I'm through with it."

Kevin took her hand. "Can I believe you?"

"Yes! I never wanted to steal. I never liked it."

"What about your friend?" I said. "Maryanne?"

"I don't know about Maryanne. I don't know why she does it."

"I don't care why Maryanne does anything," Kevin said. "I just care about you. I want to see this case closed."

Doors closed and opened in my mind. Case closed? What was our case? Was it the one Miller had filed in his notebook? The Case of the Keller Kids: Can Three Kids Make It on Their Own in the Big City? Or was it The Case of the Reluctant Taxi Driver? Or

161

The Case of the Teen-Age Shoplifter? And what was my case? The Case of the Boy Too Scared To Face Facts?

"What are we going to do with this stuff?" Kevin asked.

Lori leaned on one hand, yawning. "I'm scared. You know what I'm scared of? Maryanne will tell somebody the box is here."

"Some friend," I said.

Lori glared at me, but she didn't say anything.

"I want that stuff out of this house," Kevin said. "I want it out of here tonight."

"Maryanne said I had to keep it here."

"I don't care what she said. I don't want to see her in this house again."

"What if she tells?"

"She'll get herself in big trouble," I said.

Chapter 25

That same night Grandma Betty called and said she was coming for a visit. "Can you put up with me for a few days? I'm at the bus terminal."

"You're here? In the city? Did you tell Kevin?"

"No, why do I have to tell anyone? I just decided this morning, I had to see my grandchildren. Can Kevin pick me up in the Mercedes?"

"We sold it, Grandma. You're here? We'll come right down and get you."

"No, why should you bother? The cab's right here. I'll be there in twenty minutes."

As soon as Lori heard the news she got terribly excited and started racing around. "The house has to be clean." She dragged out the vacuum cleaner.

"Grandma will sleep in my room. I'll sleep on the floor next to her. Kevin, can I borrow your sleeping bag?" She stopped abruptly. "The box! What am I going to do with it?"

In the excitement of Grandma's call we'd forgotten it. "Put it in the back of the hall closet," Kevin said.

"Too risky," I said.

"What about the cellar?"

"No! I don't want it in the house." Lori ran out with the box. When she came back she wouldn't tell us what she'd done with it. "It's out of the house. Grandma won't see it." That's all she'd say.

"Just remember," Kevin said, "as soon as Grandma goes, the box is going." He caught her hand, held her. "And don't forget our agreement, Lori. No more stealing. No more Maryanne. Agreed? Look me in the eye, Lori. Say it."

"Okay, Kevin, okay. I get the message."

In the next half hour, we must have filled six big plastic garbage bags. Lori changed the linen on her bed and I rehung the curtains in the living room. It was a madhouse. "Grandma has to have a lamp by the bed," Lori said. She wanted her to have the TV, but it was too big for the room. Then she got worried about the way she looked and changed her clothes. "Look at me, Billy, is it on my face? Does it show? Will Grandma be able to tell what I did?"

"You look okay."

From the moment Grandma came, Lori didn't let her go. She showed her the room. "This is where you'll sleep. The bureau is for you, and the closet. I put all my stuff in Billy's room. What else do you

164

want? Do you want a snack now? Are you hungry?"

"I'm going to make supper for you children."

Having Grandma in the house was almost like having Mom back again. She set the ironing board up in the kitchen and ironed blouses and skirts for Lori, and shirts for me and Kevin that she hung on the door and the back of chairs. Every morning she braided Lori's hair and combed it out at night. And there was always a treat at supper. Gingerbread cookies one day, brownies the next. She was really lively, too, fun to be with. Every day there were domino and checkers games.

"Don't move there, Grandma," Lori said, "or I'll jump you twice."

"Am I going to lose?"

"You will if you don't pay attention, Grandma."

Grandma pulled Lori into her arms. "Umm, I love you. I'd like to take you home and keep you with me forever."

"What about me, Grandma?" I said, teasing, but liking it when she gave me the same hugs.

Grandma loved all of us, but it was special with Lori. You had to be blind not to notice. "I'm really going to miss you, honey, when I leave. I still have your room waiting."

Lori's face flushed with pleasure.

The day Grandma left, Lori was really subdued. I kept thinking everything had been perfect for three days, but who was going to take Grandma's place for Lori now? Not much to choose between Kevin and me. Neither of us were mother material. Somebody like Holly would be pretty good, but she had her own family. Mrs. Stein was too old and maybe not patient enough.

After we saw Grandma off we went across to McDonald's and sat down by a window where Kevin could keep an eye on his cab. He wanted something to eat before he went back to work. "How about getting a cheeseburger, Lori, and apple pie and coffee."

"Get me something, too, Lori." I waited till Lori walked away, then I turned to Kevin. "Kev — did you see the way Lori was with Grandma?"

"She really loves her."

"You know what I've been thinking? I think Lori should go live with Grandma Betty."

Kevin looked at me. "What, for a visit?"

"No, I mean all the time."

"Are you serious?"

I leaned forward. "She'll be happier there. Just look at the way she was these last few days. Remember the way she was before?"

"I haven't forgotten."

"She needs somebody like Mom, somebody who'll care about her and listen to her." I was impressed with myself, with how sharp I was, how perceptive, and good. "Lori's had it the hardest of all of us. She's the youngest and misses Mom the most."

Kevin removed his glasses and polished them carefully with a napkin. "You know what you're saying, don't you?"

"What do you mean?"

"You're saying she needs Grandma. But if she lives with Grandma — do you need me to live with you?"

"Well, sure, I can't live in the house alone."

"But if Lori goes, why should we even stay together?"

"Because we're a family — " I stopped, saw the trap I'd created. If Lori went, the biggest reason for us to stay together was gone.

"Well?" Kevin said.

I shook my head. I'd put my head in a noose, but I didn't want to accept the consequences. "All I'm saying is that Lori needs someone like Grandma."

"And you need someone like me to baby-sit you?"

"No, I don't need that!" If I said, Yes, I need you Kevin, it wouldn't be true. I couldn't say it. Not now, not anymore. Five months ago, after Mom and Dad died, I'd needed Kevin, all right. I'd clung to him, I was desperate for him to be home. But things had changed. I'd changed. What would a couple of years with Aunt Joan and Uncle Paul mean to me? I didn't have the right to keep Kevin out of medical school just because I thought living with them would be a little tough on me.

"Well, what do you say?"

I couldn't say it. "I don't — I want us — you, Lori, and me to stay together."

"Do you also want Lori to live with Grandma?"

"Yes. I mean — I know it's impossible — "

"Which one?"

"Both!"

Lori put the tray down. "What are you talking about?"

Kevin looked at me. "About you living with Grandma."

"Grandma! Where'd you get that idea?"

167

Kevin pointed to me.

"You want to go to Grandma, don't you?" I said reluctantly.

"When did I say that? You mean you want me to live with Grandma! You want to get rid of me, Billy. You're afraid I'm going to do it again. That's it, isn't it? You've got no confidence in me, do you? You're afraid you can't control me. You can't!" She threw a bag of French fries at me.

There were French fries in my hair, on my shirt. I picked them up one by one and put them back in the bag. "There's one in your hair," Kevin said.

Lori watched me. "Well?"

"It's not you I don't have confidence in, Lori. It's me. I've messed up your life and Kevin's enough already. What I'm saying — " I took a deep breath. "What I'm trying to say — it has to do with Mom and Dad. Everything has to do with Mom and Dad. Everything we did. Everything we didn't do. I was scared when they died. I was so scared. I was afraid to be alone, I thought it was the end, I thought we were destroyed, that there was nothing left — that's why I made Kevin come home."

"You made me?" Kevin said. "Did you ever think that maybe I did what I wanted to do when I came home? Lori's right. You don't give anybody credit, do you? You think you're the only one who cares about this family? Who appointed you God?"

"He doesn't have any faith in people," Lori said.

"You'd rather stay with us than Grandma?"

"When did I ever say anything else, Billy?"

I appealed to Kevin. "Will you tell her to slow

down? I'm not saying this because I want to get rid of her."

"Talk to me if you're going to talk to me. Don't talk over my head. I understand English."

"He's a little slow, Lori," Kevin said. "He doesn't get it that I've stayed of my free will, too."

"Have you?" I said.

"How many times do I have to tell you?"

I was getting it. It was coming at me, like waves breaking over me. I'd been sitting here for the past hour trying to do something I didn't want to do. Trying to send Lori away, which was going to break us up, and afraid every second that I'd succeed. "Are we staying together then? I always wanted us to be a family — "

"We are a family," Kevin said. "That's what I'm trying to tell you. What are we if we're not a family? Sure, we've had problems, plenty of them, and made mistakes, plenty of those, too. So what? That's the way a family works. Hey!" He looked at his watch. "I've got to get going."

He drove us home. I was quiet, still catching up, still a little dazed. I looked out the window. For months I'd been living on edge, thinking that every crisis was it. The end. No more Kellers. Every time something bad happened, I thought I'd have to pack my suitcase. And then we'd patch things up and go on.

On our street, Kevin waved good-bye. "See you guys."

"Hold it, Kev." I reached in and hugged him. "Don't drive like a maniac for once."

Chapter 26

Late Monday afternoon, Kevin parked his cab near the side entrance of Chigley's. In the backseat, Lori and I had the sealed box between us. We had agreed that I was going to "deliver" the box to the store. Kevin had wanted to do it, but Lori and I wouldn't let him. "You're too old. If you get caught it could be really serious."

"I don't want you to get caught, either."

"I won't be. But if you see me running, take off. Don't pick me up."

"I should do it," Lori said.

"No!" we both yelled.

"Don't say anything and don't run," Kevin said, and then for the tenth time he told me exactly where to deliver the box. Earlier, he'd checked out the store himself. "They take deliveries in the back, right past the furniture department. Just walk in like it's a normal delivery, hand it to somebody who works in the store, and walk out."

"Okay, I get it." The delay, the preparation, all the talk was making me jumpy. "Let's do it and get it over with."

In the store, I stood uncertainly by a side door, looking for the furniture department. "Can I help you?" a man in a gray suit said. He had a flower in his lapel and could have been a salesman or a manager, but he smelled like security. "Is that a return?" he said. I nodded and he pointed toward the back of the store.

I started down the aisle, walking slowly, not daring to look back. Was I walking too slowly? Everything in me was screaming to drop the box and run. Keep moving. Keep moving. I went past pots and kitchen wares, then curtains and rugs. Furniture and delivery were all the way over on the other side. I put the box down near a saleswoman who was busy with a customer, then bent to tie my sneaker. The man in the gray suit was nowhere in sight. I pushed the box closer to the counter and walked out of the store.

In the cab driving home, I leaned over the front seat. "Go, Kevin. Let's get out of here. You're crawling."

"Nobody's following us. Relax, everything's okay."

Lori pulled me back and rubbed my hands. "You're cold, Billy, both your hands. Was it bad?"

"No — yes. I'm just glad it's over with. Next time

you do something clever like this, you can bring it back yourself."

"I should have gone in the store. If you'd been caught — " She slumped down next to me. "Billy — do you think I made Mom and Dad ashamed?"

I shook my head.

"I did, you know I did. I feel ashamed."

"It's what happened to Mom and Dad that made you do it. Things like that can make you crazy."

"I know, I know, I know." And she started to cry.

Chapter 27

They must have it by now," Lori said the next day. We were all upstairs tearing up the damaged kitchen floor where the water had buckled it. I pried up a corner of the plywood. The new plywood was in the hall. Uncle Paul had loaned us the money to replace the kitchen floor.

Lori put down the crowbar. "What if I left something of my own in the box?" She must have said it a dozen times. It got to all of us. It was like one shoe had dropped and we were waiting for the other one to fall on us.

Lori made me so nervous that that night I actually went back to Chigley's to check. A dumb thing to do. I didn't tell Kevin. The only careful thing I did was wait till it was dark and the store was busy. The box was gone and I got out of there fast.

The three of us worked all through the weekend, nailing down the plywood. The vinyl people were coming in first thing that week. The apartment was coming together. A couple of nights we did nothing but paint. We had music and sent out for food.

Miller called one day and gave us a scare when he said he wanted to talk to all three of us. "It'll just take a minute." What did that mean? Was that how long it would take to put handcuffs on us?

False alarm! Sighs of relief. All he needed were some routine forms filled out. Afterward, he hung around to talk in his down-home way. He asked Kevin a lot of questions about the taxi job and the kind of characters he ran into late at night. Miller would have made a good DA. Before he left, Lori and I showed him the upstairs apartment. "It looks good," he said.

I was trying to give Lori more attention than I had before. I was only good at it sometimes. Morning was my prime time.

"What will it be?" I said to Lori at breakfast.

"What will what be?"

"What do you want to eat?"

"Since when are you making my breakfast?"

"From now on. Anything you want." Mom always made breakfast in the morning.

She fell right in with that. "French toast. No, make it two sunny-side eggs. And not too squooshy."

We went to school together, talked about the day

174

on the bus. Where were we going to meet afterward? What were we going to do? When it didn't rain, we went over to the playground and shot baskets. Sometimes Kevin joined us.

I still got uneasy when I saw Maryanne. What did Lori think about her? Did she still like her? Not that I said it to Lori. It would show a lack of confidence and I was trying to be careful about that. Lori said Maryanne knew about us returning the stolen stuff, so she must have talked to her, but they were through being friends. When I saw Maryanne around school I gave her plenty of dirty looks and she gave them right back to me.

One day, Lori said, "Maryanne wants me to come over to her house tomorrow."

"What did you say?"

"I told her I didn't know."

"You should have told her to forget it. You're not interested in her."

Lori pulled her hair across her face.

"You're not going to start up with her again, are you, Lori?"

"I said I don't know."

"What about Sam?"

"You keep saying Sam. I can't make Sam be my friend. If you like Sam so much, you go be friends with her. Maryanne says she's through with stores. She says it's not exciting anymore. It bores her."

"Great," I said, "what's the next excitement going to be, holding up banks?"

Afterward I told myself I had done it all wrong again. I should have let Lori talk instead of jumping

175

in with guns blazing. Let her talk. It wasn't easy for her, not having a friend.

I talked to Sam in school one day and invited her to come over to the playground and play basketball with Lori and me. It looked like it was going to be a disaster at first. The minute Sam appeared Lori stiffened up. She shot the ball to me, then I shot it to Sam.

We started playing two on one, shifting sides. When they were two against me they began to loosen up, working the ball back and forth between them to get it past me. Afterward I said, "I thought it worked out fine, Lor, didn't you?"

"Yes, God."

The bickering between Lori and me never stopped. Maybe we were together too much. Being nice all the time was too much for me. Not natural.

One day Lori said she was going to make a cake. "I'll help," I said. "Let's make the coconut chocolate Mom used to make."

"Stay out, Billy. You're not telling me what to do." She wouldn't let me come in the kitchen.

I could smell the cake baking. "Smells good," I yelled through the door. But when I saw the cake, it was a disaster. Burned on the outside and caved-in in the middle. "It looks like a bomb hit it," I said.

"Take a long walk for yourself, Billy." She took the cake and threw it in the garbage.

"Hey, what'd you do that for?" I took it out. "It's not that bad," I said, breaking off a piece. "I like a slightly burned taste. Burned lava loaf," I said, breaking off another piece. "A new sensation."

"I can't do anything right."

"Sure you can."

"I can't! And don't patronize me." She threw the glass she was holding against the wall. "I told you to stay out."

Here it comes, I thought. We're back to zero. I can't handle this. Something was wrong with Lori and I didn't know what to do. For a minute everything turned sour for me and all I could think was that this was it, the end.

Calm down, I told myself. So what if the cake fell and Lori got frustrated and you said the wrong thing as usual? So what? So you yelled at each other. That's what happened in families.

Lori started to clean up the glass and cut her hand. She swore and wiped the blood on her sleeve.

I handed her a napkin. "Put this over it before you bleed to death."

"I don't need your help," she said, but she let me bandage her finger.

Chapter 28

W hat do you want to do, guys?" Kevin said, bouncing around us in his gray sweat suit. It was Sunday morning, the first week of summer vacation, and the three of us were down by the river. Lori sat on a bench in her red gym shorts, shielding her eyes from the sun. Tomorrow she was going to visit Grandma Betty for a month and I was going to start work part-time at the CYO on the broom and mop detail. And what about the apartment? Holly and Steve moved up there, and we rented the basement apartment to the first couple who saw it. We still had to pay back Uncle Paul, but he was willing to wait, especially when he heard Kevin wanted to go to summer school full-time. Kevin wasn't going to have an easy summer. He was still going to hold down his taxi job part-time. By some miracle they still wanted him.

"It's too windy to sit around," Kevin said. "Let's jog."

"It's too windy to jog," I said.

Lori sat up on the back of the bench and retied the red bandana around her head. The shadow of her legs stretched across the path. I moved so my shadow touched hers. "What do you want to do then, Billy?" she said.

I pulled Dad's hat down over my eyes. "I'm happy sitting right here."

Lori and Kevin started down the path. "We'll wake you up when we get back," Lori called.

I watched her and Kevin till they were out of sight. All morning I'd been thinking about my parents. There was a time when I thought I'd never get over the hurt, never forget, never lose the pain. It was hard to do anything, hard to keep going. But you keep doing things even when you don't feel anything . . . you keep doing what you have to do.

You don't lose the grief. You live with the loss, but gradually — you're hardly aware it's happening — something new grows. You've lived through it. You know you've lived through it and you're all right. And that makes you feel good. What you remember is how wonderful they were.

I sat back on the bench, watching two girls standing nearby. One wore a short skirt and sandals and a raspberry-colored vest. She had strong white legs. Her friend — was it her sister? — wore jeans and a skimpy blouse that showed her middle. The one in the skirt and vest looked like a gypsy, except she was blond. A blond gypsy. She reminded me of Margaret.

The wind wound a newspaper around my leg. I saw part of a headline — PLANE HIJACKED. I kicked the paper away.

By the water a woman was feeding the gulls, throwing down scraps of bread. The gulls, on pilings and in the air, dove for them, fighting over every scrap. A plane passed high overhead and I was suddenly sure, beyond doubt, with a tightening in my throat and heart that they were here, on that plane.

Reality returned slowly. I didn't want to give up the feeling, the flush of hope and excitement, the heat in my lips. Would it always be like this? When I least expected it — when the phone rang or a door opened — caught again in the thread of hope, tightening, then loosening.

The parkway was packed with cars. In the playground, kids screamed like birds. A couple came rapidly toward me, still too far away to see clearly. They were running side by side. I stood up as they approached. *Mom and Dad. . . .* The wind weighed against my raised arms. The couple, in matching green gym suits, ran past.

I pulled Dad's hat down over one eye. A white motor launch moved hard up the river. Gulls rose into the wind. A time comes when you have to stop waiting, when you have to say, They're not coming home. They're never coming home. Nothing will work — not yelling, not tears, not ordering them back. No one will save you, there's no one to blame, no one to hide behind. Whatever you do or don't do,

180

it's never going to bring them home. There is a point when you know it's over. You're not angry anymore, you're not feeling sorry for yourself, you're not blaming them for not being there.

On the water, a long, flat, raftlike boat was coming, its wake widening like an arrow. The light changed and where the sky met the river it broadened into a white, wide, unseamed silence that slowly crossed the sky. The light was everywhere.

At the edge of the water I took off Dad's hat and spun it out over the river. *Here's your hat, Dad. . . .*

The hat sailed out like a Frisbee, then fell into the water. The gulls swarmed over it, but they soon abandoned it. Turning slowly, the hat was caught in the current and I watched it get smaller and smaller.

I glanced at the girls. The blond gypsy, the one in the short skirt, was looking at me. I tried out a smile on her.

About the Author

Harry Mazer is one of today's most popular authors for young adults. His many books include *The Last Mission; The Island Keeper;* and *I Love You, Stupid,* all of which were named Best Books for Young Adults by the American Library Association. He is the co-author, with his wife Norma Fox Mazer, of *The Solid Gold Kid* (also an ALA Best Book for Young Adults), and has most recently published *Hey, Kid! Does She Love Me?*

Harry Mazer is the father of four children. He and his wife live in Jamesville, New York.